A BODY IN
THE VILLA

Isabella Bassett

CONTENTS

Title Page

Copyright

Chapter 1   1

Chapter 2   9

Chapter 3   17

Chapter 4   22

Chapter 5   28

Chapter 6   34

Chapter 7   39

Chapter 8   44

Chapter 9   52

Chapter 10   59

Chapter 11   67

Chapter 12   73

Chapter 13   79

Chapter 14   88

Chapter 15   97

Chapter 16   104

Chapter 17   111

Chapter 18   119

Chapter 19   130

Chapter 20   136

Chapter 21   143

Chapter 22   151

Chapter 23   161

Chapter 24   171

Chapter 25   177

Chapter 26   183

Chapter 27   190

Chapter 28   197

Chapter 29   204

Chapter 30   211

Chapter 31   219

Thank you for reading A Body in the Villa   232

MORE BOOKS BY ISABELLA BASSETT: 234

CHAPTER 1

Switzerland, 1925

A hard ball of apprehension sat at the pit of my stomach, while the jaunty little bus, unencumbered by the rather desolate topography of naked rocks and jagged peaks, chugged merrily along the mountain path.

I was on my way to Locarno to join up with my Uncle Albert, whose secretary I'd recently become.

Though I was perfectly well provided for, my reluctance to share my fortune with a husband had prompted my mother to relegate me to the care of a male relation. Whether Uncle Albert possessed the acumen to tend to himself, much less to me, was a matter she had conveniently overlooked. But it was not my position that I dreaded. In fact, I'd begun to feel a certain kind of affinity towards my uncle, much like the bond forged among soldiers in battle.

I dreaded something else entirely.

While I had visited Switzerland on a few occasions before, most notably to attend Frau Baumgartnerhoff's finishing school, I had never been to the southern part of the country, where Locarno was located.

Separated from the rest of Switzerland by the Alps, the south was shrouded in something of a mythical cloak.

The fairytale status was mostly due to the south's fabled sunny weather. Whereas the rest of the country huddled under rain and snow for a considerable part of the year, it was rumored that the south enjoyed a Mediterranean climate. Until a train tunnel was bored through the deep bowels of the Alps in 1882, the only way for a pallid northerner to confirm said rumor was to go over one of the soaring mountain passes in a horse-drawn cart.

It was one of these mountain passes that I was now attempting to cross, having first left behind civilization, then the tree line, and finally any sign of life—except for the occasional circling vulture—hours ago.

I tried to calm down my nerves and reminded myself of all the beauty that surrounded me. It was mid-June, and the Alps were glorious.

Early spring into mid-summer had to be the prettiest time of the year in Switzerland. Tall mountain peaks stood out against the clear blue sky; boundless meadows undulated softly under a cover of green velvet; wild flowers danced gently in the breeze; and sheep and cows grazed serenely.

Plus, instead of a horse-drawn diligence, I

found myself conveyed in the comfort of a bright yellow motor omnibus, introduced to mountain routes by the Swiss postal service just three years ago.

I breathed in the fresh mountain air that rushed through the open top of the cabriolet omnibus. The sun warmed my face, and the wind whispered in my hair. Even the flies, which had accompanied us for a good part of the journey, after we had picked them up while motoring past some grazing cows, had by now abandoned us.

But one fly remained—the one stuck in the proverbial ointment. And when the driver announced that the San Bernardino mountain pass was only a few minutes away, he put his finger right on the fly. The ball in the pit of my stomach tightened.

Perhaps I had swallowed said fly, and it was now giving me indigestion? But I knew that not to be so.

I sighed and consulted the guidebook in my lap, yet again, but perceived no change in the text. The author of *A Handbook for Travellers to Switzerland*, a Mr. Baedeker, was resolute. He informed me—somewhat gleefully, I felt—that to reach the San Bernardino summit, one first had to endure sixteen serpentine turns up the mountain's steep side. As I steeled my stomach, I pondered the displeasing fact that even such modern conveniences as motorcoaches could not evade the realities of ascending mountains.

We paused at the top of the pass for a few minutes, and as I drew in deep breaths, I dragged my mind away from the pit of my stomach and to the sublime scenery encircling us. Snow-covered peaks and majestic mountains stretched far into the hazy-blue distance. I felt as though I were standing atop a mighty bastion. Behind me was German-speaking Switzerland, and everything I knew of this country, and ahead of me lay the mysterious lands of the Italian-speakers.

What awaited on the other side?

A sharp whistle from the driver put an end to my musings, and he ushered us back on the motorcoach.

As though emboldened by the proximity of our destination, the driver now plunged the omnibus down the mountainside in a manner no different from a child riding a toboggan on first snow. Negotiating a series of complicated zigzags bringing us to the valley below with far less regard than I would have afforded them, the driver's only concession to the rules of the road was an occasional merry "toot-toot" from his horn when approaching blind turns. The warning proved to be of limited use to several hapless vehicles caught in the wave of our perilous approach.

The merry omnibus breezed on unhampered.

"Rather!" Poppy exclaimed next to me as the valley now opened up before us. It was the first time she had spoken in a long while, and I was not certain if she was relishing in the driver's alacrity or commenting on the view. On either side of us, waterfall cascades galloped down the cliffs, as though racing with our omnibus.

After our adventure on Lake Garda, Poppy and I had seized the first opportunity to leave Italy, and had crossed over the Alps into Switzerland. Though we had never been bosom friends, and though I had considered her an implacable bully while she had been Head Girl at Boughton Monchelsea School for Girls where we had gone to school, recent events had forced us to grow closer.

We had thus spent the past few weeks traveling through this charming country. Starting off with a visit to Frau Baumgartnerhoff's establishment, we had then made our way across valleys, meadows and mountains, overnighting sometimes in mountain huts run by the Women Swiss Alpine Club and other times at tidy pensions operated by a network of Swiss divorcees like Frau Baumgartnerhoff herself.

We'd had a marvelous time, spending the days with only a rucksack on our backs, rambling through flower-strewn meadows, and meeting cows grazing high up in the mountains, their cowbells providing a soothing rhythm as we hiked. We traveled mostly by rail, but sometimes caught these new motor omnibuses.

For much of our present ride, while I had

been rendered speechless with nausea, Poppy had been engrossed in the new Leica 35mm photo camera which she had acquired in St. Moritz. As small as one's hand, as sleek as an evening bag, and decorated with silver knobs, buttons and a silver-rimmed lens, it was apparently one of the first specimens to leave the factory. Perpetually on the lookout for the latest fashion, Poppy's determination to have the apparatus was somewhat tempered by the camera's German provenance. In the end, the camera's exorbitant price, which only made it more attractive, had tipped the scales.

Poppy had proceeded to spend the rest of our trip working her way through the film inside the camera, and I suspected she only piped up now because she had run out of frames. She was fiddling with the knobs in a haphazard but confident manner, and I was afraid that she would expose all her frames to the sun and lose her hard-won record of the majestic Alpine landscape.

Our omnibus driver, on the other hand, appeared unmoved by the scenery. Instead, he spent most of his time looking backward, speaking to the passengers over his shoulder—regaling us with anecdotes of mountain climbing accidents and vehicles flying off cliffs—switching to look forward only when necessary to negotiate the next turn. My stomach protested violently.

Putting her spent photo camera aside, Poppy

turned her attention to me. "Where are the members of the Royal Society congregating again?" she asked, referring to the Royal Society for Natural History Appreciation, of which my uncle was a member. The Society, whose membership was colonized almost exclusively by peers of the realm, had a tendency to travel *en masse* to foreign places in the name of surveying curious coleopterans and the like.

I took a deep breath to calm my stomach into submission, lest it should use the opportunity to demonstrate its disapproval of the trip, before answering. "They are staying at a villa in Locarno, belonging to one of the Society's members. But the object of their interest is located somewhere near there, at a place called Monte Verita," I said.

"Truth Mountain?" she said, translating the name for herself. "Sounds ominous."

"Yes, the name does conjure images of hair-shirts in one's mind," I said in half-jest.

Poppy laughed. "Do you think they'll be indulging in self-flagellation?"

"I hope not. Though, I got the impression, from what Uncle Albert said, that the place is run by pious monks. So it's possible," I conceded.

With my uncle, one could never be entirely certain what to expect.

"What would the Society want with a place like that?" Poppy asked.

"Apparently it's the current quarters of some

ISABELLA BASSETT

ISABELLA BASSETT

rare specimen of bird," I said, and shook my head.

"It all sounds rather dull," said Poppy.

I nodded. Although my uncle had promised the diversion of a Midsummer ball, I brooded over exactly how *rather dull* the weeks ahead appeared.

I examined my thoughts critically. Was something else making me unsettled besides the omnibus ride? Was it apprehension? Or was it rather a secret wish that the monotony of secretarial work would be punctuated by the type of catastrophic misadventures of which Uncle Albert had proven himself to be a harbinger?

Whatever the cause of my disquiet, I concluded, there wasn't much hope of an adventure at a place named Truth Mountain.

CHAPTER 2

After changing trains twice, Poppy and I arrived at our destination.

The excitement of Italy had proven to be too much for my uncle as well, and he had elected to give the flora and fauna of England a closer look. But a word from Switzerland, from one of the honorary members of the Royal Society, had roused him and the rest of the members into descending upon the unsuspecting town of Locarno.

I was surprised to discover that Locarno was a pleasant little town with elegant Italian palazzos, stylish cafes, and narrow cobbled stone streets. It was situated on the shores of Lake Maggiore, with Italy just visible across the water in the distance.

Something of a connoisseur of public transport, having spent many jolly hours utilizing the transport maze of London while playing amusing scavenger hunt games with my chums, I was glad to see that Locarno possessed an adequate supply of railed vehicles, quite proportionate to its size. A small blue tram traversed the town and a blue funicular ferried passengers from the center of town up to villas in the cool hills above.

After settling into our accommodations at the Grand Hotel, Poppy and I parted company for the day.

Poppy, who had not abandoned her dream of owning a villa on the Continent, drew up a plan of attack and, lured by promises of everlasting summers, went in search of a property along the shores of Lake Maggiore. I made my way to Uncle Albert, who was staying at a villa above town.

The funicular afforded me a bird's-eye view of Locarno and I delighted in the vista of red rooftops, palm trees, exuberant blooms and the sparkling lake.

The villa where my uncle, along with the rest of the Royal Society, currently resided, offered a similar prospect of town and lake. In keeping with its Italianate style, tall palm trees flanked the highly ornamented ochre facade. The inside was equally Italianate with frescos, cornices, and other decorative moldings. It was as though I were back in the villa in Italy, I mused with a shudder.

After I was shown to his rooms, Uncle Albert and I exchanged pleasantries and briefed each other on events of the past few weeks. Despite the slightly wooly gaze in his eyes, my uncle appeared in good health. A requisite uniform of a fez atop of his downy tufts of white hair and a velvet smoking jacket round his stooped frame, was complemented by a natural history volume affixed securely to his lap.

"So why has the Royal Society decamped to Locarno?" I turned to my aging relation. I knew his ornithological interests had brought him here, but was uncertain of the details. The members of the Royal Society tended to have the most harebrained contests and rivalries related to animals and plants.

"Lord Dodsworth received a communication from the fellow whose villa we're in, Mr. Linnaeus, about the most wonderful bird nesting in an undergrowth, up above a fishing village in the vicinity," he said, waving an arthritic hand uncertainly all around him.

"What's the bird, uncle?" I asked, intrigued. I had already been to the South of France on the trail of an obscure orchid, and to Italy to observe the opening of a capricious flower, so I wondered what this exotic bird could be.

"Oh, it's a rare beauty!" Uncle Albert gushed. "A Baillon's crake, *Zapornia pusilla*. A highly secretive creature. Spends most of the time in the undergrowth of bushes. Shy, you see. Usually one can only hear it—has the call of a frog. But it's a notoriously difficult chap to observe. It hasn't been seen nesting in England since the spring of 1851, when Lord Mantelbury's great uncle managed to shoot the last suspected breeding pair, which had taken up residence near a marshy patch on his Sneaton estate, mistaking it for grouse. So when we got word that the fellow had been observed in Switzerland—what was the name again of the village, Wilford?" he turned to his erudite valet who was standing straight-backed by his elbow, ready to be of service.

"Ascona, My Lord," Wilford supplied.

"Ah, yes. I knew it was something Shakespearean," my uncle replied and turned his attention back to me. "So when we got word of an unconfirmed *Zapornia pusilla* sighting, of course every member of the Society was most anxious to come and be the first to make the definitive observation."

A mischievous grin passed over Uncle Albert's lips, and I could see him wiggling his toes in his tasseled slippers. "Lord Whatley and I have a little wager riding on who will spot the bird first," he said, and adjusted the fez at a rakish slant, no doubt to emphasize his confidence in his own assured success. "Show Caroline the bird, Wilford."

For a moment, I thought my uncle had the bird in a cage with him, or worse, had a stuffed specimen of it. I'd had quite enough of stuffed animals for a while.

The Golden Platypus—the stuffed specimen embodying the Royal Society's most coveted annual prize—which my uncle had won in France and then proceeded to misplace in Italy, was now, most sensibly, locked in a vault deep beneath the Bank of England. My uncle basked in the certainty that it enjoyed the same impenetrable security as the bank's gold ingots, on top of which he had personally placed it.

But instead of a bird, Wilford handed me a somber book, a monograph titled *The Natural Habitat and Habits of <u>Zapornia pusilla</u>*. I leafed through the pages of the slim volume, but the book's inward disappointment echoed its cover. Having expected an arresting and showy bird, I was forced to consider that perhaps the publisher in London had run out of ink.

"Is this it?" I questioned my uncle, as I flipped back to the front of the monograph.

My tone was perhaps more pointed than was polite, but once again I questioned not only my uncle's sanity, but that of the entire Royal Society. They had proven time and again that when it came to Nature, there was no accounting for what the members found attractive or interesting.

Staring at me from the lithograph on the title page was a small brownish bird with a hunched back (if birds could have that!), small eyes and an ordinary beak.

I turned the lithograph towards my uncle. "And *this* is the admirable specimen you're after?" I reiterated.

"Yes, yes," my uncle nodded excitedly, bouncing slightly in his seat. "Above the village of...at that mountain..." he faltered. My uncle was not to be relied upon for names outside the realm of Nature.

"Above the village of Ascona, My Lord. At Monte Verita," Wilford offered.

Uncle Albert nodded again.

Deciding to abandon the merits of the bird as a lost cause, I instead turned to the name which had caught my curiosity. "What kind of place is this Monte Verita?" I asked.

"The Society's members haven't visited yet," my uncle said. "Even Mr. Linnaeus consented to postpone the pleasure until we had all arrived. But I imagine it's a sort of monastery. I am told the village boasts a Catholic seminary, so this is perhaps some ecclesiastical offshoot, given the sanctimonious name...Apparently vegetarian and living in harmony with nature..." He delivered this with the same vagueness he bestowed on all things unrelated to natural history. "Sounds quite austere," he added with a shiver.

I had to agree with him. Monte Verita sounded less and less appealing. I began to wonder if women were even allowed to set foot on this sacred mound.

Uncle Albert cast a hazy gaze in the distance, as though trying to pin down the wisp of an ephemeral thought. "There was something else about the place," he added with squinting eyes after a pause, "though I can't quite recall what that was...it seemed significant...I'm sure it will come to me."

Out of the corner of my eye I got the impression

that Wilford was endeavoring to suppress a smile, but by the time I turned my head, his face had assumed its customary expression akin to the death mask of some revered Victorian composer or other.

"So who is this Mr. Linnaeus?" I asked, changing tack again. I had never heard him mentioned.

"An industrialist. A Swede. But a good amateur ornithologist nonetheless," my uncle said. I didn't quite see why Mr. Linnaeus would have desired to be a member of the Royal Society, but concluded that news of the Society's feats had not quite reached the shores of Sweden. "Mr. Linnaeus had been in correspondence with one of the monks at Monte Verita, when the monk wrote to tell him about the Baillon's crake," my uncle added.

As we spoke more about the latest mission, it transpired that the event had brought out all the Society's most illustrious members: Lord Abington; Lord Fetherly, my uncle's biggest rival; Lord Mantelbury and his dull personal secretary Alistair; Lord Packenham and his rather dashing personal secretary James; and had even occasioned the addition of Lord Whatley and Lord Dodsworth.

The delegation was undeniably quite substantial. But the conversation with my uncle had left me even more uncertain over why the Lords of the Royal Society had traveled to Switzerland to look at a brown bird at a monastery.

I would have to wait until the following

day, however, when a visit to Monte Verita was planned, to satisfy my growing curiosity and see the bird for myself. For now, I positioned myself at the desk in my uncle's room and began going through his correspondence.

CHAPTER 3

The assembly that set off the next morning from Mr. Linnaeus' villa for Monte Verita was a sight to behold. If the local authorities had possessed any inkling as to the extent of preparations taken on by the Royal Society for its visit to the monastery, and if they had been of an enterprising inclination, they could have sold theater tickets. But as it were, only a few passersby were fortunate enough to witness the spectacle.

I wagered that Mr. Linnaeus, who had been called away to Zurich on some urgent business, would regret missing the outing once he'd heard about it from his neighbors.

In the first rays of the day, the Lords, their personal secretaries and, in some cases, their valets had gathered to await conveyance to Monte Verita. As it was generally understood among the members of the Society that the community they were about to visit was quite austere, the Lords had taken the precaution to bring with them everything they might need. Front and center was the paraphernalia necessary for observing the brown bird—binoculars, stands, spotting scopes, umbrellas, sun tents, folding chairs, loungers, plus books ranging from general volumes on birds of Switzerland, to more specialized volumes dealing with migratory birds of Southern Switzerland, to specific monographs of the Baillon's crake. The more artistically inclined among the members (and who wasn't?) had packed easels, paints and sketchbooks. Along with a fortnight's supply of food and drink, I also spotted a daguerreotype camera and, inexplicably, a dictaphone. I suspected that Lord Mantelbury's secretary, Alistair, was responsible for that particular inanity, but didn't press the point.

In the end, a rambling caravan of donkeys and carts, recruited for the task from several local villages, set off to transport the Royal Society to Monte Verita.

A band to accompany the sendoff would not have been amiss.

While the rest of the Society's private secretaries departed with their employers, I was saved from an early start by Wilford, who offered to accompany my uncle on the ordeal up the mountain in my stead. I was to join them later.

I waved the caravan off and took the funicular down to the town's center, where I joined Poppy for breakfast in one of the Italian cafes.

As Locarno was not proving to be quite fashionable enough for Poppy in her quest for a villa, and as she had heard that Ascona was a charming fishing village popular with the avant-garde Continental set, Poppy decided to join me on my excursion up to Monte Verita after breakfast.

A motorcoach transported us from Locarno across the river to Ascona, where we were told that the only way to reach the community of Monte Verita was by a donkey cart.

Thus, we found ourselves rattling along a mule trail towards Monte Verita. I wondered vaguely about how backwards a place must be if one could not reach it by a motor car.

It seemed our driver was equally unhappy about having to convey us to Monte Verita. I could pick out the monastery's name amongst his incessant mumblings, accompanied by the occasional spitting. I wondered what had occasioned his obvious dislike for the place. Was he not a religious man? Did he not approve of the way the brothers lived their lives? Reminding myself that most of the locals were Catholics, I concluded that perhaps the community was Protestant.

As we slowly rose higher over the village of Ascona, I noted that it looked much like the other villages in the area—small gray stone houses with gray slate roofs crowded along the shore of the lake and huddled around a stone belltower in the center. The only charm emanated from the rows of vineyards that girdled the village. Despite the Mediterranean climate, there was an air of destitution about these villages.

They were so unlike the ones we had seen in German-speaking Switzerland. Those villages had displayed prosperity, even affluence, with wide houses decorated with intricate woodwork and red flowers spilling out of window boxes, and fronted by well-organized gardens.

The donkey cart slowed down as we reached the summit.

The first clue that the monastery might not be as expected came from the gate that greeted us at the entrance. The driver jumped out of his cart and swung open a curved white gate, designed in the modern art deco style. As the cart crossed the threshold, whimsical lettering across the gate post announced that we had arrived at Monte Verita.

But even if I had heeded the gate's warning, it would not have prepared me for what awaited me inside. The driver cursed under his breath and crossed himself. I understood his concern.

It was a scene better suited for a painting by the celebrated artist Hieronymus Bosch than a monastery. The only image that kept floating up in my mind was the *Garden of Earthly Delights*, which I had seen at the Museo del Prado in Madrid.

Poppy and I stepped gingerly out of the cart and onto a large meadow. We had instinctively come to hold hands.

At one end, a group of people, men and women, danced around in a circle. It wasn't their loose, long hair—the men as well—crowned with floral wreaths that I found slightly surprising. It was that they were all dancing around completely naked.

"The *Danse Macabre*," Poppy breathed out.

I nodded, rendered speechless.

An unkind thought, like a worm in an apple, began making its way through my mind. Was the bird truly the reason the Lords had traveled here?

I turned my head to the other end of the meadow and was rewarded by an even more unnatural scene.

There stood the distinguished Lords of the Royal Society, lined in a semicircle. All seven Lords, in somber morning suits, were bent at the waist, gazing intently through binoculars poised on stands in front of them.

But here was the surprising part—in true Royal Society for Natural History Appreciation fashion, each Lord had his back firmly turned away from the alluring visions of the dancing troupe and binoculars squarely trained on the undergrowth of a small, dry shrub.

CHAPTER 4

Even by the low standards set forth by my uncle, owing mostly to his customary vagueness on any topic beyond beetles, his intelligence regarding Monte Verita was a spectacular failure.

While it was true that he had communicated some details about the community with accuracy —the residents followed an austere way of life, were vegetarians and communed with nature—he had misunderstood completely the true essence of the establishment we were visiting.

Monte Verita was not a monastery or a religious community replete with pious monks. It was a bohemian enclave.

Wilford summed up my uncle's folly as he leaned towards me and whispered, "Your uncle forgot about the disrobed women, My Lady."

I nodded. Wilford's smirk from this morning now became clear. I also surmised the reason behind his offer to accompany my uncle to Monte Verita.

I had long suspected that Wilford was a student of human nature and its many forms of folly. While the Royal Society afforded ample material, Monte Verita promised to be just as fertile ground for study.

As Wilford seemed the most informed out of our company on the subject of the commune, I pressed him to tell me more.

It transpired that the colony at Monte Verita was a utopian experiment set up by a group of idealists. The commune tended to attract the disillusioned offspring of the upper classes, who, finding little meaning in lounging around the cafes of the fashionable cities of Continental Europe, preferred to lounge around here, on the shores of Lake Maggiore, basking naked in the sun.

Most residents brought along sizable inheritances, which they tended to bequeath to the commune, thus ensuring that everyone within its boundaries was provided for. Some residents chose to engage in avant-garde artistic work which they then sold to other idle rich who sought to add meaning to their lives through pouring money into radical thought and experimental art.

Gathered at the commune were anarchists, expressionists, nihilists and those who generally enjoyed dancing around naked. As word of the community had spread across Europe, it had also started attracting writers, artists, dancers, philosophers and anyone who was anti-establishment.

"One could say the residents of Monte Verita are experimenting with a new social order," Wilford said. "But I suspect most residents are here to escape the expectations and responsibilities that inherited wealth brings."

Scrutinizing the spectacle around me, I could not understand how the Lords of the Royal Society had failed so completely to grasp the nature of Monte Verita prior to their visit. But judging by their continued fascination with the undergrowth of the small shrub and the complete disregard for anything else around them, perhaps the Lords had not noticed that anything was amiss at Monte Verita.

One could not say the same about the private secretaries and the valets. These had gathered in groups, and, sweating profusely, were attempting to avoid even the slightest glance towards the local residents. I tried to catch James' eye, but he seemed to be engaged in something very important, having to do with a book.

My eyes glided over the contours of his handsome face and I noticed his ears were a delightful shade of red. Even the skin under his floppy blond hair seemed to be blushing. James had been my brother Charles' closest friend. Charles had died in the Great War. James and I were chums, and I often got the impression that he wanted to be more than chums. Or perhaps that was just me.

I shook my head to dislodge thoughts of James. I surmised that now was not an opportune moment to tease him.

And anyhow, I was here to be my uncle's secretary. But as I looked around, I determined that there wasn't much for me to do at the moment. So I joined Wilford in his study of the commune.

Beyond the large meadow, small wooden cottages were scattered. And further still were visible the rows of vineyards and orchards.

Having performed their morning ritual, the residents were now attired in white robes. Unencumbered by the Lords' presence, they went about their day, the sun's rays filtering freely through their vestments. Young women, about my age of 25, sat around in a circle and made fresh floral wreaths. Others practiced innovative dance moves. Old men, in long white beards and wrinkled skin, attired simply in a white loincloth, toiled away in the orchard. Younger men, also with long hair and beards, sat under the shade of trees, philosophizing.

As lunch neared, it transpired that the carts laden with the Royal Society's food and drink for the day had mysteriously disappeared along the way to Monte Verita. No amount of enquiring drew any sense out of the villagers who had conveyed the Society to the commune and were now idling around, waiting to drive the Lords back to Locarno in the afternoon. Questions from the Lords' secretaries were answered with hands thrown towards Heaven, as though the vanishing of the provisions was an act of God.

"One can only hope the local villagers will appreciate the bottle of 1907 Maison Euvy champagne," I said to Poppy, referring to the exquisite bottle from Lord Whatley's private reserve that had gone the way of the provisions, "as much as the Lords claim they would have."

The generous souls of Monte Verita, learning of the Royal Society's predicament, pranced around in their loose clothes and set up a long wooden table with a cornucopia of Nature's local bounty—strawberries, cherries, peaches, honey, dry bread, and acetic wine.

The Lords gaped at the feast, but as there was no other sustenance to be had, they joined the commune's residents at the table. The valets hovered behind their employers, ready to slice a peach or a plum at a moment's notice. Not a single word was exchanged during the meal and only a grudging thank-you was offered at the end of lunch by the Lords. I quite enjoyed myself. I believe Wilford did as well.

Following lunch, Poppy and I returned to our sun loungers. The Lords returned to their mysterious bird, which I gathered no one had managed to spot just yet. And the personal secretaries and valets returned to huddling around the Lords. I had seen none of them so hard at work—taking notes; adjusting binocular stands, or chairs, or chair pillows; and offering to clean the lenses of the binoculars with a soft cloth. In fact, they all appeared desperate to avoid looking in the direction of the Monte Verita commune, whose members were now sunbathing on the meadow in various states of undress.

A gentle breeze swayed the tall summer grass, bees buzzed, leaves rustled, birds chirped, and the gurgling sound of a stream flowing nearby filled the air.

As the afternoon progressed, the sounds of summer seemed to lull the guests into a slumber —some were dozing in loungers, some on blankets on the warm grass. Perhaps the place had a magical quality to it, after all.

But a noise somewhere far away threatened to unsettle the peace. Loud voices, quite at odds with the purported utopia, carried over the medley of summer sounds. And as the voices got nearer, I gently lifted an eyelid to observe the arguing party. So jarring was the disturbance that, after a moment, I could not help but open both eyes and watch the unfolding drama under the cover of the brim of my sunhat.

CHAPTER 5

A casual observer would have concluded that I, like Poppy, was napping, exhausted by the afternoon sun. But in fact, after trying to catch Poppy's eye, but finding her asleep, I had proceeded to observe the disagreement closely.

A party of three had approached the meadow. A quick glance told me they had not joined us for lunch. As though unaware of, or untroubled by, the presence of the Royal Society, they continued their quarrel unchecked.

The arguing party comprised two young men—one fair, one dark—and a young woman, perhaps younger than me by a couple of years. Judging by their appearance, they were recent additions to the commune. They lacked the unkempt look of the long-term residents of Monte Verita, though all three had taken advantage of the informal dress code and attired in breezy white clothes.

The woman was clearly agitated and was shouting at the fair man. "There is no such thing," she said. "You are completely wrong." She turned on her heel and walked further on. The two men followed her.

"Emmeline," the fair man called after her,

pleading. Tall and strapping, he had no trouble catching up with her in one leap. She paused. He pulled her gently towards him and turned her to face him. He cradled her face in his large hands. "Darling," he said, gazing at her face, "I didn't mean anything by it. Please, forgive me."

Emmeline turned demurely away from him, but did not flee from him this time.

My glance traveled to the third of their party. This man was more slender, though no less athletic in build. And no less handsome. His wire-frame glasses and dark hair swept artistically to the side, gave him the look of a poet.

The burning look in his eyes was unmistakable —he was consumed by a desire for the woman. Or was that a look of hatred directed at the fair-haired man kissing Emmeline? As the sun reflected off his lenses, it was hard to tell.

But what was clear was that I was witnessing not only a lovers' quarrel, but perhaps even a lovers' triangle.

The woman named Emmeline had a tragic beauty about her, as though she were the heroine out of Sir Walter Scott's *The Lady of the Lake*. Or was I thinking of the *La Belle Dame sans Merci* by Keats? Either way, she had a beauty that gave one the impression that, like a siren, she drew men in with dire consequences.

Her hair was long, her foot was light, and her eyes were wild, I quoted to myself.

Not only that, but she also had a trim figure, which she had emphasized by tying a braided belt about her narrow waist with a bohemian knot.

Perhaps school boys brought up on a steady diet of Romantic poetry cannot help but fall in love with her, I mused. For not only her two companions, but now another young man was standing in the background, staring fiercely at her.

For a moment I thought the man was staring past Emmeline, but when I turned I only saw Lord Packenham.

Lord Packenham—a stuffy old egg—seemed just as taken in by Emmeline as everyone else. And perhaps I was not the only one who thought Emmeline was the personification of Keats' ballad. Lord Packenham appeared paler than usual, and, if I didn't know better, I would have said that he wore the look of having seen a ghost. *La Belle Dame sans Merci thee hath in thrall*, I mused.

Poppy stirred next to me, sat up, and interrupted my reflections. "Rather! Isn't that Emmeline Walpole-Semperton?" she asked enthusiastically.

I shrugged. I did not know who the young woman was.

"By Jove! What luck! It is! What is she doing here, I wonder?" Poppy started to get up, but I pulled her back.

"Who is she?" I asked, intrigued by the effect this Emmeline seemed to have on a remarkable portion of the men at Monte Verita.

"Why, don't you know?" Poppy turned to me in amazement. "Well, perhaps not," she reconsidered. "Your lot doesn't go in for the families of industrialists."

She was right. Though my mother was the daughter of an American industrialist, having married an English Earl, she had made it her mission for our family to socialize only with other titled families. This narrowed the pool of victims for my mother's dinners considerably, and left most titled families across the British Isles, and some on the Continent, living in fear of receiving a summons from my mother. This they were helpless to refuse, lest their social stock should degrade.

Poppy's family, on the other hand, was full of well-to-do industrialists who had discovered, or improved on, a staggering amount of industrial methods and machines, and had built a fair number of bridges to boot. They tended to socialize with other such families.

"Emmeline is the heiress of the Walpole-Semperton fortune," Poppy said in a conspiratorial whisper. "Her father invented some industrial method or other. Terribly clever invention, but I can't remember what it was at the moment. But something went wrong, as far as I remember. Some accident or other. Some people died or got sick....Or was it actually her uncle...Regardless, there was a scandal about some explosion...or a flood in a mine...I can't remember. In any case, it was something like that." She concluded her surprisingly uninformative piece of gossip with a wave of her hand, as though to dismiss it. "Families had to be compensated...but I'm sure she's well provided for."

Having thus exhausted the topic of Emmeline's fortune and its provenance, Poppy rose out of her lounger and went to join her.

"Emmeline!" she yelled out to her and pushed the fair man out of the way. He started to protest, but upon perceiving Poppy's girth and determination reconsidered and turned his attention to me.

After introducing himself as Spencer, he enquired about the purpose of our visit to Monte Verita. He was exceedingly diverted by my description of the Royal Society's current task.

"So you are not here to join the commune?" he said, and smiled. Everything about him was radiant: his smile, his tan, his golden hair. "It's not to everyone's liking," he said, looking around and throwing a furtive glance at Emmeline, as though afraid that she would overhear.

From her bored expression and the way she kept looking past her, I got the impression that Emmeline was not interested in renewing her acquaintance with Poppy. But Poppy seemed not to notice.

As I threw a casual glance in the direction of James, I noticed that he was watching me.

"Then you must join us for a day at the beach in Ascona," Spencer was saying. I realized I had not been paying attention to him. "It's so nice to see some new faces. Perhaps you can join us tomorrow," he said. "All the young men can come, if they want to." He glanced in James' direction.

"I'm not sure how many of us could be spared," I said without jest. The Lords seemed to be quite devoted to their bird watching task and might require a great deal of lens polishing. I wondered if Lord Packenham could do without James for a day.

"I hope you can make it," Spencer said with a child-like eagerness. "There is a Swedish chap with a fast boat on the lake, one of those new sleek runabouts, and he lets us use it for waterskiing."

Waterskiing! Now there was something I had never tried.

CHAPTER 6

The powerful motorboat roared back and forth across the lake as we watched from the short pier. I had taken up Spencer's offer for a beach day in Ascona.

Spencer, gliding on water skis in the boat's wake, waved towards us. He tried out different tricks, lifting first one leg and then the other. He had tied his skis to his feet, so they would not slip off, in order to perform these antics.

Having tried waterskiing this morning, I appreciated how much body strength he needed to hang on to the rope and keep himself upright, let alone lift his skis.

The lake water had been freezing as I had waited for the boat to pull me forward—my feet attached to the two wooden skis by a leather strap —but I'd hardly felt its temperature. As I'd watched the slack rope floating on the surface of the water uncoil, and had readied myself for the rope to yank me forward and out of the water, excitement had coursed through my body, keeping me warm. Plus, James had been watching from the pier.

Waterskiing had turned out to be much like aquaplaning, except that instead of gliding across the water on one solid board, one's feet were placed on two planks somewhat wider than snow skis. My ride, while short-lived, had been pure exhilaration.

Poppy was also determined to showcase her own athletic prowess in front of so many handsome young men, and was awaiting her turn eagerly. James, Alistair and a few other of the secretaries had seized the opportunity of a beach day to escape the mortification of Monte Verita. Some local boys had joined us, Spencer having promised to let them have a go on the skis. And the spectacle had drawn more than a few curious onlookers. We were all sitting along the pier, dangling our feet over the water.

Emmeline was standing a bit to the side of the group. She was watching intently as Nicholas, Spencer's dark-haired rival for her affections, was driving the boat and dragging Spencer around the surface of the water at an ever greater speed.

Spencer and Nicholas had proven to be expert waterskiers, having spent most of the summer practicing on the lake. And they had taken turns to give me a few quick lessons—which had amounted to "lean back" and "keep your tips up"—on the beach before letting me try waterskiing.

Although I had found Spencer's company quite pleasant yesterday, I discovered this morning that Nicholas was the more charming of the two. No wonder Emmeline seemed to have trouble making up her mind. While Spencer was energetic and unencumbered, Nicholas proved to be gallant, sophisticated and worldly. He had a way with words that lured one in. His deep brown eyes, with a mischievous twinkle, were just as enticing. His suave manner could rival that of a confidence trickster, I'd mused.

Spencer's candid laughter carried across the water and over the motor's roar as Nicholas turned the boat around sharply. Nicholas was driving the boat ever faster and Spencer reveled in the challenge. He attempted small jumps in the boat's wake.

We cheered him on from the pier.

At the rate Nicholas was driving, they would soon reach the islands visible in the middle of the lake.

Then, the engine cut off, and the motorboat halted abruptly. Spencer coasted on the water for a few moments and then began to sink. He was making some signals to Nicholas, but it was hard to see what they were from our spot on the beach. I wished I had a pair of binoculars with me.

Now they were shouting at each other, but I could not make out why that was. Nicholas seemed to be trying to start the boat again, but it would not start. Spencer was swimming towards the boat, but his feet, tied to the skis, were slowing him down. Nicholas pulled at the rope to get Spencer back on the boat.

Suddenly, as Spencer neared the stern of the

boat, a struggle erupted. It was so difficult to tell from my vantage point what caused it.

"What is going on?" Emmeline screeched unexpectedly from behind us.

In the blink of an eye, the situation had changed. The two men were screaming at each other and splashing water about.

"What is that young man doing?" asked Alistair. I wasn't sure if he was referring to Spencer or Nicholas. Neither seemed to be acting soundly.

"I think Nicholas is having trouble pulling Spencer back onto the boat," said Emmeline. "He's trying to lift him out of the water, but he can't." She looked around, fear in her eyes. "Someone, do something. Go and help him!" she screamed.

We looked along the beach, but there were no other boats to be had. The fishing boats in the old harbor were far away. James and some of the other secretaries began running in the direction of the fishing boats.

I turned my attention back to the water. In the few moments I was turned away, something had happened. Spencer was no longer visible in the water by the stern. Nicholas was checking the sides of the boat, as though looking for Spencer.

"What's happened?" Emmeline screamed. She grabbed my arm, her fingernails digging into my skin. I was uncertain about what had happened. It looked as though Spencer had gone under the water's surface, but I did not want to tell her that.

"Where is Spencer? I can't see Spencer!" she cried out.

Now more people had gathered around us. Nicholas was moving frantically from bow to stern, from port to starboard, making the boat rock. It was clear that he had lost sight of Spencer.

I glanced towards James. Having reached the old port, he and the secretaries were now rowing in the direction of the motorboat.

From the pier, we watched, helplessly, as they rowed around the motorboat, Nicholas shouting instructions at them. But after a while, Nicholas climbed into the fishing boat and they rowed back to the shore.

CHAPTER 7

Nicholas climbed onto the pier with difficulty. He was as pale as a ghost. Emmeline pounced on him like a tigress. "What happened?" she asked. "Where is Spencer?" She was holding him by the shoulders, shaking him. Some of the secretaries tried to pull her back.

"There was nothing he could do..." someone was saying, perhaps James.

"But where is Spencer?" Emmeline looked around frantically, as though expecting him to be among the secretaries. "What happened?" she yelled at Nicholas. "Tell me what happened!" she now screamed.

As though unable to keep his balance, he sat down on the planks of the pier before answering her. "I'm not really sure," he said, looking around in a daze. "I had him...he was under my hands..." He glared at his hands, as though he was trying to make sense of what had happened. "But he just disappeared...just slipped away from under my hands."

"What do you mean he just disappeared?" Emeline shrieked, leaning menacingly over him. Her voice carried a hint of panic and urgency.

"Were you not holding on to him?"

Nicholas' eyes shot up to hers. "Yes, I was, Emmeline!" he snapped at her. He seemed to have recovered from his momentary stupor. "But somehow, while he was under the water, he just sank. Like a stone," he said in an abrupt manner.

"How could he just slip away like that?" she asked, now almost frantic. She began pacing back and forth on the pier. I had a feeling she had forgotten that the rest of us were here. Onlookers stepped back, out of her way. "Did he drown?" she asked, turning again to Nicholas.

He looked up at her and studied her for a moment. "I think so," he said. But uncertainty filled the space of his pause. "I've never seen a person drown before, Emmeline."

"Did you not see him under the water?" she pressed on. "Did you not see his body under the water?" The note of urgency had returned to her voice.

"It was all so sudden," he replied. "In the panic....water was splashing everywhere, the waves...I could not see. Plus, I was trying to keep my own self in the boat. In his struggle, Spencer was going to pull me under as well."

Emmeline halted and looked down at Nicholas. "What have you done?" she breathed out the question.

He shook his head and buried his face in his hands. "I did what I could," he said. "It was all I could do before he disappeared."

Emmeline looked away from him and gazed in the distance to where the silent motorboat bobbed on the water. Nicholas got up heavily and joined her. They stood there together, side by side, in silence.

But after a moment, she turned to him. "How could you?" she snapped at Nicholas and stalked off.

That night, I kept going over what had happened at the beach.

My own experiment with waterskiing had ended abruptly when my skis got caught in the boat's wake and I lost balance. But as I had started sinking, it had been easy to slip my feet out from under the straps of the skis. I also had no difficulty swimming up to the boat once I was free of the skis.

What had happened to Spencer? Why had he not been able to get back into the waiting boat? By all accounts, Spencer was a strong swimmer.

Perhaps Spencer's problem was that he had insisted on tying the skis to his ankles with additional leather straps. Planning on attempting some acrobatics, he didn't want the skis to fall off his feet.

Had his skis caught on something underwater?

Lake weed? Fishing nets? Had the skis prevented him from getting back on the boat?

The police had arrived not long after the accident, and a boat had gone out to search the water. A diver had examined the lake near the motorboat, but no body was found. The only thing the police had been able to recover was one of the skis. It was seen floating on top of the water some distance down the lake, the current having carried it further in.

The police and the villagers, who had experience with this sort of thing, concluded that the body would wash ashore in a few days. The most likely cause of the drowning, they explained, was a current. They tried to console Emmeline by telling her that sometimes strong currents formed in the lake for unknown reasons, and pulled even good swimmers down to a watery grave.

Neither the police nor the villagers seemed particularly surprised by the drowning. For them, it was a regular occurrence. The lake waters were treacherous, and the calm surface belied the strong currents beneath.

And yet, there was something that troubled me. Why had Nicholas not been able to pull Spencer back onto the boat? I had seen Nicholas attempt to help his friend. But there was so much violence in that rescue. It was as though Nicholas was fighting against a force that was pulling Spencer down. Watching from the shore, it had seemed as though a monster had taken hold of Spencer's legs and was dragging him down against all his will.

I shook my head at the absurd idea.

Something Emmeline had said floated up in my mind—is that how people drowned? Did they just drop off?

And what about the one ski? Why had it come off Spencer's foot? And where was the second ski? Was it still attached to Spencer's body?

I sat upright in my bed. *Of course!* What if the scene was not as it appeared?

What if Spencer's skis had caught on something, like lake plants or a fisherman's net? The trap, perhaps aided by a strong current, had pulled him down and away from the boat. That would explain why Nicholas could not bring Spencer up. And it would explain why I had seen a struggle. The two men were struggling against the current that was pulling Spencer's bound feet.

Then perhaps Spencer dove to undo the straps of his skis, to release his feet from the trap. That would explain why he had gone under water suddenly, why he had slipped away from under Nicholas' hands—he'd plunged to untie his skis.

But why had he not come back up?

The single ski recovered, I feared, provided an unhappy clue. Spencer had drowned while trying to untie his skis, managing to free his feet from only one of them before running out of air.

CHAPTER 8

Upon hearing of the drowning, my uncle had chastised me for taking part in what he called "wild shenanigans". Though he had never censured any of my activities, the unfamiliarity of waterskiing must have given him a jolt, because he went as far as to give me some sage advice. "Good food and wholesome fun. That's the ticket," Uncle Albert had said. "One can't drown rowing a boat, that's what I say."

The drowning weighed heavily on my mind as well. But it did not prevent me from planning to attend the Midsummer ball at Mr. Linnaeus' villa that evening. After all, it was one of the few pleasures this trip promised.

I spent a subdued day at Monte Verita. The residents kept mostly to themselves, and Nicholas and Emmeline were nowhere to be seen. Perhaps they were giving statements to the police. The Royal Society passed the day at the edge of the meadow, transfixed by the dry shrub, and ended the day's outing on a low note, having failed to spot the retiring bird for a third day in a row.

I began to suspect that there was no bird there at all, but my uncle assured me that he had heard a distinctive croak. He dismissed my suggestion that perhaps it was indeed a frog vehemently.

One could only hope that the ball this evening would lift everyone's spirits.

Although I had been to his villa several times now, and we had used his motorboat with such tragic consequences yesterday, I still hadn't met Mr. Linnaeus in person. But based on my uncle's description of the circumstances behind his admission to the Royal Society, I could not wait to make his acquaintance.

According to Uncle Albert, Mr. Linnaeus had been admitted to the Royal Society because the Society's members had believed him to be a descendent of Carl Linnaeus.

"The father of taxonomy and binomial nomenclature," my uncle explained. "To have such a scion as a member would have been a great triumph and a matter of distinct pride for the Royal Society," he concluded.

While in due course it had been revealed that the Society had been mistaken in their belief, the revelation did not come before the members had pursued poor Mr. Linnaeus for two years, trying to persuade him to join their organization.

"In the Royal Society's defense," my uncle said, "in addition to his duplicitous name, Mr. Linnaeus resided in the city of Uppsala!"

The members had further fooled themselves into thinking that Mr. Linnaeus was their man because Uppsala, regrettably, also happened to be Carl Linnaeus' *Alma Mater*. Thus, several Royal Society delegations had been dispatched to Uppsala in pursuit of Mr. Linnaeus' membership.

"Further delegations were sent to Mr. Linnaeus' countryside residence in Smaland," my uncle added, with a sorrowful shake of his head.

At first, Mr. Linnaeus had tried to explain to the Royal Society's delegations that they were mistaken in his identity. But as they took no notice of his objections, and attributed them to a commendable display of modesty, and as it seemed they would not relent until he was a member, Mr. Linnaeus finally acquiesced to their requests.

Soon after Mr. Linnaeus began attending the Royal Society's meetings, however, it became apparent that, unlike his purported ancestor, he had little interest in botany or zoology.

"Though he does possess some rudimentary interest in birds," my uncle acknowledged grudgingly. "But his interests run more along mechanical lines. He's an industrialist," my uncle whispered. "And apparently, he is an enthusiastic collector of fast cars and boats." My uncle's tone betrayed his scorn for such diversions.

But having pursued him so relentlessly for two years, the Royal Society was reluctant to revoke his membership, lest the members had to admit their mistake. And for his part, Mr. Linnaeus did not want to disappoint the members, who had spent so much time convincing him to join the Society, by submitting his resignation.

With time, Mr. Linnaeus and the other members of the Society had found a mutual ground. The English Lords had discovered the beauty of the Swedish countryside in summer and all its attendant insects. And Mr. Linnaeus had come to appreciate the Lords' connections with British politicians and industrialists.

Tonight's ball was in the Swedish tradition of celebrating midsummer's eve. It was to be a masquerade, and given the celebration's pagan roots, and in honor of the Royal Society, Mr. Linnaeus had decreed that the theme of the masquerade was to be Nature.

Uncle Albert was quite excited by the idea, and spent a fair amount of time considering his costume options, before settling on going dressed as Dr. Livingstone. He considered it the only decorous costume for a person of his standing.

Poppy and I had opted for more inspired interpretations of the theme. She was going dressed as her namesake, Persephone, and I was to be dressed as a woodland sprite.

We had chartered a car to convey us from the hotel to the villa, and I was waiting by the vehicle as Poppy emerged from the hotel, dressed in a black evening gown. The only nod she had made to the goddess of spring was a floral wreath in her hair.

"What happened to the sheet?" I asked. Poppy had planned to use a white sheet to complete her Grecian ensemble. She mumbled something which sounded suspiciously like not finding a sheet wide enough to encompass her girth.

Poppy's frame ran to the proportions of a linen closet, and it was a testament to the skill of couturiers in Paris that she usually looked quite fashionable and elegant. I conceded that the white sheet would not have been an appropriate look for her.

"And what about you?" she asked, eying my own failed costume gleefully.

"Any attempt to make fairy wings ended up in disaster," I said and shrugged, which made the two palm fronds attached to the straps of my own black gown rustle apathetically.

As the car tires crunched on the gravel of the villa's driveway, my spirits lifted. I could already tell that this was to be a proper party, and regretted not putting a bit more effort into my costume.

Fire torches lined the driveway and directed the way to the villa. Insects chirped loudly in the warm evening air.

A magical summer night was descending over Locarno. Below us, yellow electric lights flickered on in the small town of Locarno. It seemed as though hundreds of fireflies had come to life. The lights reflected in the dark lake, and the ripples across its surface made the lights wink.

Elegant couples alighted at the grand portico from elegant cars. Everyone had taken the dress code to heart and wonderful interpretations of the nature theme paraded in front of us. Posies of woodland nymphs and sprays of exotic flowers scurried into the villa, followed by hunters and birds, and even someone dressed in a full-body gorilla suit.

Once again, I regretted my choice of wings and acknowledged with a sigh that the leaves had begun to wilt.

Inside, candles flickered and green garlands fashioned out of summer foliage were strung across the rooms and wound their way up staircase railings like ivy tendrils.

The crystal light of chandeliers danced upon the champagne flowing down a stacked glass fountain inside the ballroom. And a band played pleasant classical music. I did a double-take. This was the band from the Grand Hotel. I recognized the violinist, in particular. But I knew him better as the man who played saxophone in the evenings in the Jazz band at the hotel. I wondered at the transformation.

Poppy handed me a champagne coupe, and we went in search of my uncle. My secret hope was that my uncle would be in the vicinity of the other members of the Royal Society, who, in turn, would be in the vicinity of their secretaries. In short, I was hoping to catch a glimpse of James. Though my costume was pitiful, I knew that my blonde hair shone to its best advantage under the light of chandeliers, and my dress was particularly slinky this evening.

I spotted the back of my uncle and his Dr. Livingstone-type cap, with the distinctive neck-protecting cloth tied around it. Surprisingly, my uncle was deep in conversation with Hector, the private secretary of his biggest rival at the Royal Society, Lord Fetherly.

But as I approached my uncle, I realized that this was indeed Lord Fetherly. And he was wearing my uncle's costume! Confused, I looked around, and discovered, to my amazement and amusement, that there were at least seven Dr. Livingstones scattered around the room.

I finally managed to spot my uncle and moved in his direction. The scowl on his face and the murderous looks he cast in the direction of the other Lords told me that he was not a happy man this evening. The glamor, lights and elegance were lost on him. He only had eyes for his rivals.

"What-ho, Uncle Albert," I chirped, in an attempt to cheer him up.

He only grunted in reply and threw a disparaging look in the direction of Lord Mantelbury at the far end of the room. I was delighted to see that Alistair, his secretary, had dressed as Stevenson—recognizable by his pith helmet—to complement Lord Mantelbury's own interpretation of Dr. Livingstone.

"What happened, uncle?" I said. "Why is everyone from the Royal Society dressed like Dr. Livingstone?"

"I haven't the foggiest," he replied testily.

"Did you tell anyone about your costume?" I asked, trying to get to the bottom of the mystery of the seven Dr. Livingstones.

I wondered whether in the future the Royal Society should treat masquerades like debutante balls—gown designs kept in strict confidence and dressmakers sworn to secrecy.

"No, I did not," he said with a fiery fervor and threw a blazing glance at Lord Dodsworth idling in the western corner of the room.

It was clear that I wasn't going to get anything else out of my uncle on the matter, and proceeded to presume that despite knowing the precise binomial nomenclature for each of the six reptile species native to the British Isles, when confronted with the task of dressing for a masquerade, and deprived of their wives' guidance, the Lords of the Royal Society lacked the imagination to dress in anything beyond Dr. Livingstone.

I looked around for James, in the hopes that he could elucidate the enigma. But while I was looking for him in the crowd, I spotted an unexpected guest. And as the guest moved out of the way, I spotted a second.

CHAPTER 9

There, in the middle of the hall, dressed in a resplendent costume, looking like some exotic butterfly, stood Emmeline. And next to her was Nicholas—easily recognizable despite his Greenman mask of leaves.

What are they doing here?

Wasn't the opulence and excess of the Midsummer ball in stark contrast to everything that the community at Monte Verita stood for? Gone were Emmeline's bohemian garbs, replaced instead by sumptuous silk layers. Her dress was exquisite and extravagant. It was a cross between what one would wear for the dance of the seven veils and Loie Fuller's infamous dress—the one with all the fabric flapping around her as she danced.

If I hadn't met Emmeline and Nicholas at the Monte Verita community, I would not have paid them any attention. They looked like many other guests at the ball, drinking champagne and enjoying themselves. But their presence here seemed not only out of character, given their residence at Monte Verita, but also in poor taste, given Spencer's drowning. Was Emmeline not devastated by Spencer's loss?

Who had invited them here? And for what purpose?

James interrupted my thoughts, as he joined Poppy and me, and then led us to meet the host. He was dressed as a London Zoo attendant.

"Incidentally," I said to James as he guided us through the crowd, "do you know why all the Lords are dressed like Dr. Livingstone?"

"I'm not certain about the others, but Lord Packenham declared that it was the only decorous costume for a person of his standing," he said and smiled.

I laughed. "So did Uncle Albert!" James joined in.

His eyes twinkled mischievously as they glided over my face. His smile was bewitching and I smiled radiantly back. His eyes then slid down to the wilted palm fronds protruding from my shoulders, and the momentary spell was broken. He was too much of a gentleman to comment, though he gave me a quizzical look.

Mr. Linnaeus, when we were introduced, turned out to be a nondescript, middle-aged man. He looked much like any MP currently sitting in the House of Commons—of middling height, hair parted in the middle, body thickened through the midriff.

He seemed a nice enough man and had taken the Royal Society's current ornithological inclination to heart. He was dressed like Papageno from Mozart's *The Magic Flute*, complete with feathers, pipes, bells and a birdcage.

"I'm delighted you recognize it, Lady Caroline," he said when I complimented him on his costume. His evident delight suggested that few other people had understood it. "It pains me to say that the Lords of the Royal Society completely misunderstood my costume. Once they had mistakenly identified me as the Greek god Hermes, I could not alter their belief," he said, and laughed good-naturedly. Perhaps the feathers had confused them, I considered.

Mr. Linnaeus seemed to be taking the folly of the Royal Society in stride, and I spent a few more minutes engaged in a pleasant exchange with him.

But as he moved away to greet another guest, I turned my attention back to the two visitors from Monte Verita. I surveyed the party until I located them. They had moved somewhat to the side and appeared to be less cheerful than before.

I wondered what had precipitated the change and moved in their direction, feigning a need for a champagne refill. Hovering behind some potted plants, blending in rather well thanks to my wings, I was well within earshot of Emmeline and Nicholas.

"I know what I saw," Emmeline hissed at Nicholas.

"We shouldn't have come. Do you want to

leave?" said Nicholas. "You are not feeling well."

"I'm quite well," she snapped. "I know what I saw," she said, though less assuredly. "I must be going mad," she concluded, speaking almost to herself.

"It could not be him, Emmeline," Nicholas said gently. "It's just your imagination."

She pulled away from him and looked around. "I'm telling you, he's here."

"That's impossible, Emmeline." Nicholas moved closer to her.

"I'm sure of what I saw," she snapped at him.

"And what was that?" he said, a note of mocking in his voice. "A reflection in the mirror that was gone when you turned around?"

"I'm frightened…" she whispered.

"Of what?" he asked.

"Of ghosts. Magda says that such things can happen. Spirits are real. And Monte Verita sits on a powerful energy line…it draws the spirits in—"

"Enough. Let's get you a drink," he said, and pulled her towards the drinks table.

I stood behind the potted palm tree for a few moments.

What had Emmeline seen? A ghost? Spencer's ghost?

I looked around the room. There were quite a few men with light hair and athletic builds—the lake seemed to attract the athletic type. Anyone of them could have looked like Spencer for a moment. Especially in the reflection of a mirror.

But why would she be frightened of Spencer's ghost?

I grabbed a new champagne coupe and one for Poppy and rejoined her.

Then, as the clock struck midnight, the orchestra performed a magic trick. Up until then, they had been playing a series of waltzes and some light marches, to the delight of all men past the prime of their lives. But at the last stroke of the clock, a piano was rolled in, the violinist I had recognized earlier put aside his instrument and picked up a saxophone, the cellist did the same and took charge of a drum kit, and thus rearranged they struck up James P. Johnson's *The Charleston*. They had become a proper jazz band.

The junior constituents of the crowd whooped and cheered, and a frantic waving of hands and legs ensued. Poppy and I were some of the most enthusiastic dancers, with petals and leaves flying everywhere. The agitation seemed to be too much for my fronds, and they finally came off. I was glad to see James also join in, though with a somewhat subdued exuberance. And even Alistair, Hector and the other private secretaries were bobbing along to the intoxicating rhythm.

The seven Dr. Livingstones seemed to have put aside their mutual animosity and had formed a dissenting semi-circle, goggling at the dancers.

While Uncle Albert was tapping his foot merrily, Lord Packenham wore an expression that gave one the idea that he was about to telegraph Lady Packenham to make sure their daughter, Winifred, did not engage in any such outrageous behavior. Unbeknownst to Lord Packenham, however, Winifred, known as "Wild-Winnie" to her friends, was one of the most enthusiastic participants in the recent all-night dance contests at her London club.

The more progressive of the older guests, overcoming their initial shock, now sidled cautiously into the thick of the fray. I spotted our host, Mr. Linnaeus, on the edge of the crowd, looking as though needing a soft nudge to join us. Since he had been so enlightened as to engage the jazz band from the Grand Hotel, I thought it only fitting that he should join in on the fun. I grabbed his hand and dragged him into our little group. At first he protested, but then spent a diverting half-hour with us as Poppy and I tried to teach him the Charleston steps. He was an enthusiastic student, though not very talented. And though his bird-catcher costume seemed to be something of a hindrance, the bells added greatly to the gaiety.

But the fun came to what felt like a screeching halt. The band ended a song and was about to start another when we heard a scream. At first I thought that someone from the band had fallen off the stage, as I'd seen happen before, or a dancer had fainted from exhaustion. I'd seen that too, though never Winifred.

Then the shriek came again, and it was not from the ballroom. It was from somewhere deep in the house.

The guests fumbled for a moment, unsure what to do. But when the scream came a third time, we all moved as one towards its source. Mr. Linnaeus pushed his way through the crowd and led the way, bells jingling. We followed him down one corridor and then another.

The woman who had screamed crumbled as she saw the approaching guests. Someone grabbed her under the elbow to steady her and led her away. As she departed, we turned our attention to that which had caused her to scream.

There, lying on the floor, wrapped awkwardly in her layers, was Emmeline.

At first, it looked as though she had just fainted. There was a large electric fan behind her. One could be excused for thinking that perhaps she had come here to cool herself down and fainted from exhaustion.

But at a second glance, the layers wrapped around Emmeline's throat made it clear that she had been strangled. And what was even more disturbing was that it looked as though she had been choked to death by her own dress, caught in the electric fan.

CHAPTER 10

I followed the end of the cloth with my eyes. It was wrapped around the blades of the electric fan. It looked as though the blades had twisted Emmeline's shawl until they had throttled her. And once they had done that, the tension had brought the fan blades to a stop.

Mr. Linnaeus reached towards Emmeline as though to free her from the fabric cutting into her neck.

"No, don't touch her!" someone from the crowd cautioned. "The police would have to be called."

Mr. Linnaeus looked at the speaker, confusion flickering in his eyes. Then he seemed to recover. "Yes, of course." He looked around and, spotting one of his footmen in the back, told him to phone the police.

Silence fell over the gathered audience. In the stillness, the electric hum of the fan could be heard. The motor was still working.

"The fan," someone said. "Turn it off. It's pulling on her scarf."

A man reached down and unplugged the fan. The humming stopped, and the grip of the scarf around Emmeline's throat slackened a little.

At that moment, a man's voice came floating from the back of the crowd. "Who is it? Which young woman?" the man asked. "Let me through," he said with some force. The crowd parted for him.

It was Nicholas. "No!" he exclaimed when he saw the body. "Emmeline!" He rushed towards her. "What are you all looking at? We need to get this scarf off her, help her breathe!" He threw off his mask, rushed towards the body, and crouched down.

"No, my boy," said Mr. Linnaeus, gently placing a hand on Nicholas' shoulder and pulling him back. "There is nothing we can do for her now. We have to wait for the police."

Nicholas' body sagged under the weight of the words and he stared blankly ahead.

Mr. Linnaeus turned to his guests and spread his arms as though to usher them out of the confined space of the passageway. "There is nothing any of us can do for the poor girl now. Let us leave her here until the police arrive."

People began moving slowly away, some murmuring, some turning back to take another look at the body. I hung back. Poppy sent me a questioning look, and I gave her a meaningful glare. I wanted to stay and observe a bit more before the police arrived.

It all seemed so strange. I was trying to wrap my mind around the scarf twisted around the blades.

Something was very odd about this. Could such a thing really happen? Could a fan strangle a person? Wouldn't the air from the fan blow fabric away from it? And even if Emmeline's dress had caught on the blades, wouldn't she have enough strength to tug it free?

The passageway emptied, and soon only Poppy, Mr. Linnaeus, Nicholas and I remained. Nicholas drew a cigarette out of his cigarette case, fumbled with a shaking hand with a lighter, and cursed when he was unable to light it. Mr. Linnaeus struck a match and offered him a light.

"Go outside and get some fresh air, my boy," Mr. Linnaeus told Nicholas. Nicholas hesitated and threw a furtive look at the body. "Don't worry. I'll stay with the body," the host added.

Mr. Linnaeus leaned over the body as though examining it with his eyes and said something to himself in what sounded like Swedish. He straightened up, his bells jingling incongruously, and realized with a start that Poppy and I were still there.

"Lady Caroline!" he exclaimed. "You should join the other guests," he suggested.

"I'd like to stay with the body, if you don't mind," I said. "Emmeline was a close friend of Poppy's." Poppy threw me an alarmed look and was about to protest, but I shook my head to warn her off.

He eyed Poppy for a moment, but did not question our motives. Poppy, finding herself unable to retaliate in front of Mr. Linnaeus, instead pinched me hard on the arm. It was one of the many ruthless tactics she had employed to subdue the populace during her reign as Head Girl. I winced in pain and wanted to kick her in the shins, but restrained myself.

"You have such a kind heart, Lady Caroline," Mr. Linnaeus said. He turned to look at the body again. "Poor girl. What a tragedy for her family."

"Do you know her family, Mr. Linnaeus?" I asked, intrigued by his comment.

I didn't fail to notice that he cleared his throat and paused before answering, as though selecting what answer to give me. "I knew her father to a moderate degree," he finally offered. "In a professional manner," he added.

I had wondered earlier why Emmeline was at the party, and now was the perfect opportunity to ask. "Mr. Linnaeus, had Emmeline been invited to the party?" *Was it possible that she had come to the party uninvited for some reason!?*

"Yes," he answered. "I'd heard that she was staying in the area and extended an invitation to her. I invited all the residents of Monte Verita, in fact. But she, and that young man of hers, were the only ones who reciprocated by attending the party."

"The Monte Verita residents don't strike me as

fond of this particular type of gathering," I said with a smile. I had nothing against Mr. Linnaeus' party. Indeed, I had quite enjoyed myself up to this point. But the Monte Verita people gave one the impression that they were above such temporal affairs.

"Yes, I know what you mean," he said. "But I was doing my neighborly duty. Most of the people residing at Monte Verita come from excellent families, and among them are those with sharp wit and stimulating new ideas. They make fascinating conversation partners. One finds the general company of this area somewhat unvaried and conservative in their views. The Monte Verita residents are quite different." He paused for a moment. "But you are correct. Perhaps this is not their idea of a midsummer party."

Dancing naked around bonfires would be more their thing, I thought, but didn't verbalize it. I once again wondered what had made Emmeline attend this party.

Had she perhaps come to meet someone here? Or was she just a typical young woman fond of revelry in general? Perhaps she liked the idea of a midsummer party, like I did. Perhaps Poppy would have some insight, but now was not the place to ask. Not in front of Mr. Linnaeus. I didn't want him to suspect that I was "investigating".

"What a strange accident," he said, drawing my attention back to the body. "These fans are quite dangerous." He shook his head at the machine on the floor. "I wonder what this one is doing here."

"What do you mean?" I asked, perplexed.

"Well," he began with some hesitation, as though trying to recollect the order of events, "I don't remember seeing a fan here before. A few are scattered around the rooms, of course." He swept a hand to encompass the house. "With the heat of the summer, one has to take advantage of modern conveniences...Perhaps one of the footmen placed it here to create a draft. We'll know soon enough."

I wondered what had drawn Emmeline to this part of the house. When I'd overheard her conversation with Nicholas, she had been genuinely concerned about someone she'd recognized at the party. Did that person lure her here? Or had she been running away from them?

And where had Nicholas been at the time of her death?

"Where does this passageway go?" I asked.

"Nowhere in particular," Mr. Linnaeus said. "Just to my office and other such rooms. I don't know what would have made the young woman come this way? This part of the house holds no particular interest to anyone but myself."

What indeed?

The quick footsteps of several people echoed down the corridor, and I assumed the police had arrived. But when the group rounded the corner, I saw my uncle, followed closely by James.

"Ah! Young Carol!" Uncle Albert exclaimed. "You gave me such a fright!"

"What is it, uncle?" I said, concerned.

"People were talking about a young woman decapitated by the blades of an electric fan, and when you didn't come back, I thought it was you!" He leaned on the top of a small table, hand to chest, attempting to catch his breath.

"I tried to reason with him," interceded James, who had been my uncle's former secretary, and knew of his many quirks and foibles, "and to explain that you are quite well. But he insisted on coming to see for himself."

My uncle caught sight of the dead body and moved for a closer look. "Poor young woman. Dangerous things, those." He pointed at the electric fan. "Wouldn't have one of these infernal contraptions in my home," he declared. "Nearly lost a finger to one." Noticing his extended finger, he retracted it in haste.

Uncle Albert then threw an accusatory glance at Mr. Linnaeus, as though he were responsible for the girl's death by welcoming such a deadly machine into his villa. "What would your great-uncle, Carl Linnaeus, say?" he added for good measure.

James and Mr. Linnaeus at first ventured to correct my uncle's mistaken impression of Mr. Linnaeus' family lineage. But reconsidered and shook their heads at the futile task.

A fresh wave of grumbling, footsteps and raised voices traveled down the corridor towards us and announced the arrival of the police.

CHAPTER 11

Two policemen, followed by Mr. Linnaeus' butler, advanced towards us with the air of superiority adopted by petty officials who'd finally managed to catch you at a disadvantage. It was a manner I was well acquainted with, having encountered it many times displayed by constables in London while engaged in innocuous fun with my chums.

The one leading the procession was a youngish-looking chap with a crisp dark uniform, well-oiled dark hair and a well-tended mustache. His straight back and sharp eyes signaled a military background.

He was accompanied by a somewhat less dapper assistant. There was something in the demeanor of this deputy that suggested they'd endured a difficult journey. His uniform bore the signs of adventure. He was flustered and had a smudge of mud—one hoped—across his forehead, just below his cap. His uniform was splattered, and the dark discolorations at his knees suggested that he'd been recently kneeling in a fresh puddle.

The policemen excused their delay by explaining to Mr. Linnaeus that on their way here, a scoundrel had blocked the road with metal rakes placed across it, leading to a punctured tire on the official police vehicle. Thus, they had been forced to stop in the dark to change said tire. The junior policeman punctuated his superior's story with assenting nods.

I suppressed a smirk. While attending Frau Baumgartnerhoff's finishing school, I'd become accustomed to hearing about such incidents. Villagers, especially those in the mountains, enjoyed a life interrupted only by church and cow bells. They resented the noise, smoke and dust brought on by motor vehicles speeding across their quiet hamlets and took matters into their own hands.

Thus, on any given day, star-crossed travelers equipped with a motorcar could find their progress hampered by a myriad of old farming implements, rocks, tree stumps, and boards with nails strung across the communal roads. The farmers delighted in not only halting modern advancement but also in outsmarting a machine.

From the words of the policemen, it became apparent that, summoned out of a midsummer's slumber at their homes high above Locarno, they had encountered similar road impediments passing through a neighboring village.

The policemen took a few minutes to familiarize themselves with the situation—the identity of the victim, the reason she was at the party, who had discovered the body, where the corridor led, and so on.

Upon the policemen's arrival, Uncle Albert and James had returned to the hall, but Poppy and I had hung back. So far, the policeman in charge had not shown any interest in us, and I hoped our presence would go unnoticed. But presently he turned his sharp eyes on us.

"And who are you?" he asked, eying us suspiciously. He spoke English quite well, despite his accent.

"I'm Lady Caroline Beasley," I said, "and this is Miss Persephone Kettering-Thrapston."

"Poppy," she interjected. The junior policeman made the adjustment in his notepad.

"And what are you still doing here?" the senior policeman almost barked. "Why are you not with the rest of the guests?"

Just as I was deciding whether to inform the official that I was quite good at puzzles and scavenger hunts, Mr. Linnaeus intervened. "Miss Kettering-Thrapston was a friend of the dead girl," he said. I heard Poppy whimper by my side. "And Lady Caroline, as I understand," Mr. Linnaeus continued, "was waterskiing in Ascona just yesterday with the dead woman."

It was my turn to gasp. Before I could make up my mind whether Mr. Linnaeus was simply a very plain-spoken chap or had an ulterior motive for throwing us like a pair of Christians to the lions,

ISABELLA BASSETT

the senior policeman said, "What does that have to do with anything?"

The junior policeman flipped energetically through his notepad, and having located the relevant information, whispered in the other's ear.

"Ah! The young man from Monte Verita..." The senior official nodded and turned to us. "So you were present yesterday during the drowning accident?" He looked quite smug, as though he had got hold of an important lead, and made a show of pushing out his chest.

"We were," I answered. I, in turn, made sure to hold my head up high and look down my nose at him. Poppy was employing a stiff upper lip.

"I see," he said, and turned to look at Emmeline's body. "Accidents seem to plague these people from Monte Verita. All I've been hearing for two weeks is Monte Verita this and Monte Verita that. Disrupting the peace with fights and arguments with the locals. It would be better for the community if these intruders just left." He threw us a sly look. "You're not residing at Monte Verita, by any chance?"

"No!" Poppy protested, as though scandalized to be associated with such a place.

But I'd latched on to something else the policeman had said. "You think Emmeline's death was an accident?" I asked.

He did not reply, but examined my face with his sharp eyes for a few moments.

Just then, Nicholas returned from his dose of cigarettes and fresh air. Having been outdoors had done nothing to improve his appearance. He was still pale and his hair was quite limp. Emmeline's death had visibly shaken him.

"Ah, and here is the young man that was Miss Emmeline's companion this evening," Mr. Linnaeus said.

"Is that right?" The senior policeman turned his eyes like beacons on him, but didn't proceed with any other questions until the younger policeman had completed the preliminaries of taking down his name and current place of residence.

"Another Monte Verita inhabitant, I see," the senior policeman said and nodded as though that explained everything. "And can you throw some light on what happened tonight? If you were her escort this evening, how did the young woman find herself in this situation?" he asked with an accusatory note, gesturing towards the body.

Gone was Nicholas' suaveness from the previous day. *Was he frightened?* He looked around at those gathered, as though searching for a hint of the right answer. "Well," he said, after no one supplied any, "I was with Emmeline all night. As the jazz band began to play, she wanted to get a drink. I was trying to light a cigarette, and the damned lighter was playing up, so I hung back for just a moment to get it to work. And then when I looked around, she was gone. I followed her to the drinks table, where I thought she'd be, but she wasn't there. I walked around, looking for her through the crowd for a while. And then we all heard the scream. And she was just...here..." He cast a swift glance at the body and then looked away, as though he couldn't bear to see Emmeline like this.

"Do you know how she might have ended up here?" the police officer asked.

Nicholas shook his head. "I haven't a clue."

"Was she perhaps meeting someone here?" the policeman pressed on.

"I don't know..." Nicholas answered. I noticed that he was avoiding looking at the policeman.

I watched Nicholas closely and waited to see if he was going to admit to the police that Emmeline had been frightened by someone she had seen at the party.

"Actually," he began tentatively. "There is something..."

"Yes?" the senior policeman said, boring into Nicholas with his penetrating gaze. "What is it?"

The junior policeman stood in a state of readiness, frozen in the moment with his pencil poised above his notepad.

"It's strange, and I don't know if it means anything..." Nicholas faltered.

"Spit it out, man," cried Mr. Linnaeus.

CHAPTER 12

Mr. Linnaeus' outburst disconcerted Nicholas, and he took a few further minutes to collect his thoughts, during which time the senior policeman held our host in a reproachful stare.

"Well, the thing is," Nicholas began again cautiously, to the frustration of all listening, "she claimed she saw someone at the party," he said at last.

We all let out held breaths.

"Who?" asked the policeman, his eyes two slits of suspicion.

"Someone she knew," was all Nicholas offered.

The policeman was getting frustrated. "Yes, but who?" he demanded.

"She didn't say…"

I almost choked. I knew this to be a lie! I was under the clear impression that Nicholas knew exactly who Emmeline had seen this evening. Why was he not telling the police? If she had seen Spencer's ghost, or imagined to have, why was Nicholas hiding it from the police? Or had she seen someone else entirely?

"Now, look here!" The senior policeman's anger

was now evident. "Don't make me arrest you for obstructing the police! Tell me exactly what she saw and what she said. We need to identify this person."

The policeman did not say it, but I suspected he reasoned that whoever Emmeline had seen could be involved in her death.

"Emmeline didn't say who it was," Nicholas said, sticking to his story. "But I got the impression that it was someone from her past."

"A man or a woman?" asked the policeman.

Nicholas looked at him for a moment as though this was a trick question. "A man...I think," he hedged.

"Anything else? Where did she see him? When?" the policeman pressed him for details.

"She saw him during the evening, as a reflection."

"A reflection?" The policeman seemed confused, his dark eyebrows converging over his nose.

"In a mirror. In the great hall," Nicholas clarified.

The junior policeman added that detail to his notepad.

Nicholas continued. "But by the time she turned around, he was gone, hidden in the crowd. But she wasn't even sure what she had seen. And she was frightened."

"She was scared of the reflection?" the policeman clarified.

"Yes, she described it as having seen a ghost."

"A ghost, eh? Was there something untoward hidden in her past, perhaps?" the policeman said in a supercilious manner and gestured to his junior to make a note of his clever idea.

"Well, I'm not sure exactly." Nicholas appeared to be hedging again. "You see, I only recently met her...at Monte Verita."

"Is that right?" the policeman asked suspiciously. "So you didn't know her that well?"

"No, not well at all," Nicholas said.

I eyed Nicholas closely. The revelation was a surprise to me. There had been something about their manner, something about their level of intimacy that had made it appear as though they had known each other for much longer.

Nicholas, having thus distanced himself from Emmeline and her past, seemed to regain some of his color and his confidence. "And anyway," he said, "with all these costumes around, it would be quite easy for someone to hide their true identity at this party."

The policeman considered this for a moment, conceded its validity, and now turned to Poppy. "And what about you, young lady? As a close friend of Miss Emmeline, what can you tell us about her?"

Unlike Nicholas, Poppy did not seem intimidated by the policeman. Her voice boomed with assertiveness in the narrow confines of the passageway. "I knew her socially, of course. Our families know each other, though we haven't dined together in a long while. Her father and uncles are well-known industrialists."

"Her father and uncle were involved in some industrial accidents, you said," I added, reminding her.

"I don't see how that is relevant at the moment," the policeman cut me off. "We are interested in the young woman, not her father or uncle." He spoke to me in a patronizing tone, as though I were a child.

I was about to protest, and explain why the information might be relevant to the investigation, but he turned to Mr. Linnaeus. "And you, sir, was it you who invited her here tonight?"

"Yes," he answered, but did not elaborate.

"And what was your relationship with the young woman?" the policeman asked in an insinuating tone.

"I knew her father," Mr. Linnaeus replied simply. "I had extended an invitation to everyone at Monte Verita," he added.

The senior policeman shuddered at the mention of the commune. "And in what capacity did you know her father?" the policeman asked. I glared at him. Just moments before, he'd dismissed my interest in Emmeline's father.

"Professionally," Mr. Linnaeus said. "Our paths

had crossed a few years back. But as Lady Caroline suggested, Emmeline's father suffered certain business setbacks and our paths diverged."

Mr. Linnaeus was being quite enigmatic. I wondered why.

Perhaps the senior policeman thought so as well, because he asked: "What else can you tell me about her father?"

Mr. Linnaeus shrugged. "Not much. Last I heard, he was in Argentina, trying to set up new business ventures."

The policeman scrutinized him for a while, but did not press him for more information.

"So let me see if I have all the facts so far," the policeman said at last. "You, Mr. Linnaeus, invited the now dead woman to your party because at one point you were business partners with her father." I noticed a spasm pass across Mr. Linnaeus' face, but he did not correct the policeman. "She saw someone she knew, perhaps from her past, at the party. Perhaps in disguise. And it scared her. That someone lured her here to the dark corridor—"

"Or she saw them slip down this corridor and followed them," I added.

The policeman looked at me as though he didn't appreciate my contribution. "And then she's found dead," he said, turning away from me.

Although those were the facts, they somehow did not seem to grasp the whole story.

"But do you think her death was an accident,

or was she murdered?" I asked, unable to contain myself.

"Murder? Now, there is an idea," he said and gave me a long, stony stare. Then he turned to look at the fan and the scarf, as though seeing them for the first time.

CHAPTER 13

The senior policeman now turned his attention to the body. He acknowledged, however, that he could do little until the police unit from Bellinzona, the region's capital city, arrived with their photography equipment, fingerprinting kits and additional men to conduct interviews of the guests.

After muttering that he could not think what was keeping them, he proceeded to stand sentinel by the body, with a stiff straight back, until they arrived. The junior policeman, lacking his superior's confidence, shuffled nervously, and attempted to brush the mud stains off his uniform.

A footman joined Mr. Linnaeus and delivered a message to him.

"Excuse me, officer," Mr. Linnaeus said. "But a telephone message has just come through for you."

"Yes?"

"It's the police team from Bellinzona," Mr. Linnaeus said. "They have telephoned to inform you that their car has broken down. Apparently, they have met with some horseshoe nails on the road."

"Damnation!" the policeman said, losing some of his composure.

As there was little to justify our continued presence at the scene, the senior policeman ushered us away and remained with his deputy to wait for the rest of the team.

We joined the other guests, but Mr. Linnaeus, Poppy and I, having witnessed the preliminary police investigation, remained a little separated from the other guests. I had the impression that Mr. Linnaeus was just as eager as I was to discuss the case.

Nicholas moved towards a corner of the room and lit another cigarette.

"Mr. Linnaeus," I ventured, "do you think Emmeline's death was an accident?"

"What do you mean, my dear?" he asked.

"Do you think it's plausible that the scarf got caught in the blades and strangled her?"

"Your uncle seems to think so," he said and chuckled. "But to answer your question," he said and cleared his throat, "it is possible for fabric to catch on the blades. The steel blades are quite stiff, and they rotate quite fast. But you are probably right—despite appearances, the fan is perhaps too small to pull the scarf with such force as to choke anyone."

I nodded. To me it was clear that Emmeline had been strangled with her dress first and then the end of the fabric was wrapped around the fan's blades.

While I had been standing in the passageway, I had surveyed the fan as closely as I could from my vantage point. For the fabric to get sucked into the fan, the fan must have been blowing away from Emmeline, but the fan was facing towards her. The fan had been set up after she was strangled, to give her death the illusion of an accident.

But to what purpose? Why make it look like an accident when it was evident it could not have been?

"Blast it!" Poppy exclaimed next to me.

"What is it?" I asked.

"I've misplaced my camera," she said.

"Your camera?" I asked incredulously. "You brought your camera to the party?"

"Yes, and then forgot about it and wondered why my evening bag was so heavy. Then I took it out by the drinks table intending to take photos... and then with the dancing and the screams..." She moved away to look for her camera.

As people chatted around, exchanging theories about what had happened to Emmeline, I thought about who the mysterious killer could be. Was the killer the same person who Emmeline had seen earlier at the party? Was that person still here? And how could one ever find out who that person was? Everyone was in costume and some guests were even in disguise.

Poppy returned and pulled me aside. "I don't know if there is a murderer in the house, but there is definitely a thief," she said crossly.

"What do you mean?"

"Someone has pinched my camera!" she said, outraged. "It's not at the drinks table."

We informed Mr. Linnaeus, who looked mortified and enlisted the help of his footmen to retrieve the camera. But I was doubtful that any of Mr. Linnaeus' guests would have swiped it, despite Poppy's unrelenting insistence. I wondered if the more likely explanation was that Emmeline's killer, seeing the apparatus on the table, and worried that his image might have been captured among its frames, took the camera to dispose of incriminating evidence. Little did the killer know that, with Poppy not having taken any photos, there was no fear of that.

My thoughts turned to Nicholas. Why had he lied to the police that he did not know who Emmeline had seen? I thought back to the conversation I had overheard, but could not remember if Emmeline had offered any clues to the mysterious person's identity. All I could recall was Emmeline's fear of the person she had seen. Perhaps it truly was someone from her past.

And why had Nicholas been so quick to distance himself from Emmeline? Was he hiding something?

The tragic accident the day before floated

up in my mind. Were these events related? Was someone holding Emmeline responsible for Spencer's drowning? Had someone from Monte Verita disapproved of the evident lovers' triangle?

But if that was the case, should not the killer have attacked Nicholas instead of Emmeline? After all, it was he who could not rescue Spencer.

I cast a futile glance around the crowd. Was there someone else here from Monte Verita? But with so many unfamiliar people around, it was impossible to say who was here.

My eyes landed on Nicholas. *Surely, the drowning yesterday was an accident,* I thought. But what if it wasn't? Was Nicholas somehow responsible for these deaths? Was he here for revenge?

"Ay me!" Poppy signed next to me and drew me out of my thoughts.

"What is it?" I asked, suspecting she was still pining after her camera.

"He is so tragically handsome."

"Who is?"

"Nicholas," said Poppy. Apparently, she had been thinking about him as well, though in a quite different manner.

I was about to groan that Poppy had once again fallen for a tall, dark and handsome type, when a thought struck me. I looked from her to him. Poppy was just the ticket to get all the answers to my questions.

"You are right," I said.

For a moment, I debated whether to take advantage of Poppy's lack of judgment when it came to handsome men, encourage her infatuation with Nicholas, persuade her to follow him to Monte Verita, and thus send her on a mission to be my spy, without letting her in on my plan. Or whether to be a decent chum and be candid with her.

I decided on the latter. Whatever her shortcomings, Poppy was not a simpleton. She would see through my scheme right away. Plus, I suspected she would quite enjoy her double role— a femme fatale and an undercover spy.

Although men of a certain financial handicap found Poppy—or rather her fortune—attractive, Poppy was not what one would call pretty. But she was an excellent athlete, which helped her secure the company of handsome men—strong men quickly learned they could not outrun her, while the weaker ones did not even attempt to try it. She would make an excellent agent to have at Monte Verita.

"Listen, Poppy," I said to her. "How about you spend a few days at Monte Verita?"

"What? You think that will cheer gorgeous Nicholas up?" she asked, brightening right up.

"It might," I hedged. "But I also think there is something strange going on at Monte Verita. I need to have a chum in the midst there. To get inside information about Emmeline and Spencer. And even Nicholas. I need to know more about Emmeline's past, about what brought her to Monte Verita."

"Do you think there's a killer at large among the Monte Verita people?" Her eyes grew large. Whether of fear or excitement, I could not be sure.

"It's possible. I think Emmeline's death tonight is a confirmation that someone is a murderer. But I'm not sure if it's someone from Monte Verita."

"Do you think it's Nicholas?"

"I don't know. It's possible," I said. "It's certainly possible," I added after a moment's hesitation. "After all, Spencer drowned on his watch, so to speak. And now Emmeline is dead."

Poppy took a bit of time to consider things before speaking. "So let me get this straight," she said at last. "You want me to go and spend time at a place that might be harboring a murderer?"

I nodded.

"And expose myself to danger?" she asked, eyeing me with suspicion.

I nodded, but less assuredly.

"And you even suspect that the killer is Nicholas, but still want to send me there on a mission?"

Nodding seemed futile at this point.

"By Jove, I'll do it!" she exclaimed and clapped, which made a few guests turn around. "Nothing gets the blood pumping like a bit of danger." She looked hazily in the distance. "Plus, I would not be the first woman to fall in love with a criminal."

"Now, Poppy," I warned her, "you know your father would never approve of Nicholas. Especially if he's a criminal." Mr. Kettering, a decorated veteran of the Boer War, was quite protective of Poppy's fortune.

She sighed. "Yes, but one can dream…"

"And it could be a perilous mission," I added, feeling a prick of conscience to be exposing a chum to danger.

She threaded her arm through mine. "Have I ever told you about the time we went hunting on the Serengeti with Papa? I found myself surrounded by a family of hippos…"

As she prattled on about spears and war cries —all woes about stolen cameras forgotten—any doubt that I might have had about Poppy's ability to take care of herself, even in the most dire of circumstances, dissipated. Though named after a goddess that got herself abducted by a scoundrel, I had full faith in Poppy. Her disposition resembled more that of the goddess Artemis.

"Though pity about the lovely frocks I had sent down from Paris," Poppy was saying. "I wonder if Mme Lanvin could knock up a few ethereal frocks to use at Monte Verita. I better get a cable out to Paris first thing in the morning and describe the situation and the urgency to Madame…"

I knew I could count on Poppy!

CHAPTER 14

It was a few days before I could make my way to Monte Verita and check on Poppy's progress.

The police investigation into Emmeline's death took a while to make its course through all the guests who had attended the party. So it was only on the fourth day after the party at Mr. Linnaeus' villa that all members of the Royal Society—and their private secretaries—were finally free and ready to go up to Monte Verita.

The Lords went to survey the status of the bird in the undergrowth, while I went to find Poppy. Whatever I might have imagined Poppy doing at the community was not what I found her doing.

While the previous time I had visited, the members of Monte Verita were dancing around in a hedonistic fashion, now they stood lined in neat rows, like soldiers. At their head stood Poppy, dressed in some sort of Parisian couture concoction between a wood nymph and a field marshal, taking them through their morning exercise routine.

The sight brought back memories of Boughton Monchelsea School for Girls. As Head Girl, Poppy had been responsible for dragging the school's pupils each morning, regardless of temperature or weather, through a series of brisk tortures designed to invigorate us and get us mentally prepared for the day ahead. The routine had achieved neither.

By the looks on the faces of the Monte Verita residents, they were just as unhappy as we had been about the level of activity this early in the morning. But if one thing could be said about Poppy, it was that few could thwart her skills of organization and persuasion.

I waved merrily to Poppy, and she waved back, but her attention did not falter. She did not give up on her charges until all the drills were completed.

She then barreled towards me. "What ho! Good to see you, Gassy!" I cringed at my school-girl nickname, but I didn't bother to correct her.

As she came closer, I could see that a change had come over her. A casual observer would have said that Poppy was in love. And perhaps she was. She had, after all, come here to follow Nicholas, with whom she had professed to be in love. But there was a certain kind of glow emanating from Poppy that only happened when she was in charge of a complicated undertaking, with reluctant participants, that required precise organization and the command of at least three deputies. I'd seen it at school.

"How is Monte Verita treating you, Poppy?" I asked.

"Never felt better. Had our differences at the beginning," she said and threw a quick glance at the cowering populace scurrying along the edges of the great meadow, "but I think I have sorted this whole place out." She swept a regal hand across the Monte Verita domain.

I had no doubt that Poppy had managed to organize every aspect of life at Monte Verita to her liking, and in so doing had banished the very essence of the pleasure these bohemian souls had found in life at the community.

I cast a more critical eye about the place and began discerning certain changes. It was evident that Poppy and Monte Verita had come to head in a violent clash and had settled for an unhappy compromise.

Poppy had acquiesced to the demands of life at Monte Verita with a loose and ethereal frock. But it was Monte Verita that had experienced a profound transformation.

Where a few days ago tall wild grass had swayed in the morning breeze, now stood neat windrows. And where graceful nymphs had danced naked in said grass, now crisp, white linen flapped, hung on washing lines.

The breakfast table had also undergone a metamorphosis. Gone were the plates of plums and prunes, replaced by a full English breakfast.

Poppy caught me looking at the table. "I made sure to tell the milkman and butcher to make regular stops at the camp from now on. You'd hardly imagine what I found when I arrived here?" She shook her head in disbelief, but didn't wait for a reply. "Grown men living on fruits and seeds! No one had bothered to contact the milkman," she said, a note of incredulity in her voice. "No wonder everyone looked so emaciated before I got here."

I wondered how the residents had taken to this change of leadership, but I wasn't about to pry. Perhaps all this bohemian freedom had left a power void at Monte Verita that Poppy had only been too happy to fill.

"Have you been able to find out anything?" I asked, referring to the original purpose of her mission to Monte Verita.

"Not much," she admitted without timidity. "These people, although they give the impression of progressive radicals, are pretty taciturn. But to be honest, most of my days so far have been taken up with trying to get this place up and running to its full potential. I'm in negotiations with some of the local farmers to develop some of the fields…"

I let Poppy's enthusiasm for administration run its course, and I wondered if the Monte Verita residents would be more forthcoming with information if Poppy was not quite such a bully.

"And I'll tell you something else, talking to the butcher and the milkman from Ascona, I got the impression that the Monte Verita community is not well liked by the locals. The locals think they are a bunch of lunatics up here. I tend to agree with them—loose clothes, incessant dancing, and if they are not dancing, they are sitting cross-legged under trees. There's even an old man from the village who comes up here and looks over the wall, and shouts obscenities whenever he spots someone."

The policeman's words from the ball came back to me. He had also suggested that the Monte Verita residents were troublesome and disliked by the locals. I wondered if these troubles with the locals were somehow related to Emmeline's murder.

"So you have nothing to report on the matter of Emmeline?" I asked, lowering my voice, so we would not be overheard.

"There is something," she said. "They engage in something called Anthroposophy here, but I put an end to that."

"What is this anthro-something?" I asked. Sounded like some new science.

"It's a way to communicate with the spirit world," Poppy said.

I rolled my eyes, but suppressed a groan. Three of my aunts, like the witches in *Macbeth*, were quite keen on the spirit world. While their predictions were mostly correct, they were usually delivered to the wrong person. Their seances were like watching a game of pin the tail on the donkey, where, having got a hold of a piece of prophecy from beyond, they fumbled around as to which relative to pin it on.

"Adherents believe that the spiritual world is tangible and accessible and one can communicate with it," Poppy was saying. "You know how Emmeline apparently saw someone at the ball before she died? Here they believe it was a spirit trying to communicate with her."

"What makes them say that?" I asked.

"By all accounts, Emmeline was quite gifted in communicating with the spiritual world. She had seen a spirit earlier in the day, before going to the party."

"Does anyone know who she saw?"

Poppy shook her head. "They attempted to summon Emmeline's spirit after her death, but Nicholas objected most forcefully."

I wondered if it had been Nicholas' skepticism, which I had witnessed at the ball, or something else that had prompted him to stop the seance. The name Magda floated up in my mind. Emmeline had referred to her during the ball. I wondered if it would be worthwhile talking to her, but Poppy interrupted my thoughts.

"But that's just a load of balderdash," she said and waved it off. "Something more tangible has occurred," she said.

"Yes?" I asked eagerly.

"One of the residents has disappeared," Poppy said.

"Who?"

"The one they call Brother Gregor," she said.

His name held no significance for me. "Who is he?" I asked.

"The one hanging around, with the long hair and beard, on the day we met Emmeline," she said.

As she described him, a picture emerged in my mind, and I remembered the young man who had been standing in the background the day we had arrived at Monte Verita, when Spencer, Nicholas and Emmeline were having what had appeared to be a lovers' quarrel.

While I had only spared him a glance on the first day, and had not thought about him since Emmeline's murder, his behavior that day now took on a new significance. He had looked as though something had upset him. Was it the quarrel? Had he also been in love with Emmeline?

"Do you know who this Brother Gregor is?" I asked.

Poppy shrugged. "Beyond saying that he's an English chap and university educated, the residents had little else to contribute to Brother Gregor's identity."

"And when did he disappear?"

"Well, it's quite hard to tell," Poppy began. "Brother Gregor is said to be something of a recluse. Some residents claim they haven't seen him since the day the Royal Society arrived at Monte Verita. But others contend that he disappeared on the day of Emmeline's death."

"Do they think his disappearance is connected to her death?"

"No one is really sure. Apparently, Brother Gregor has a habit of going off to the mountains for days and sleeping like a hermit in caves. He has done it before."

"So no one has gone out looking for him?" I asked. "And no one has informed the police of his disappearance?" I added, incredulous.

Poppy shook her head. "No one saw the need for such drastic actions. Apparently, there is a lot of this coming and going at Monte Verita." She waved a careless hand about to illustrate her point. "People are quite free to do as they please, I am told," she added, her voice laced with outrage. "But I've decided to put an end to that and have started a truancy ledger and a chores roster in a bid to bring some sort of semblance to this place."

I suppressed a smirk, but gave a silent thanks that I didn't have to stay at Monte Verita under Poppy's command.

As I watched Poppy order the residents about, I wondered whether there was a more mundane reason for Brother Gregor's hiatus in the mountains. I shook my head. The dates did not coincide. Brother Gregor had disappeared long before Poppy took control of the commune.

But even though Brother Gregor's disappearance did not seem to bother the residents of Monte Verita, I could not help but feel that the timing of his disappearance was of significance. Why would he leave the community right after Emmeline's death?

What was more, his disappearance now made for the third strange event at Monte Verita—first Spencer's drowning, then Emmeline's death, and now Brother Gregor's disappearance.

Several questions were vying for attention in my head: Was Brother Gregor somehow involved in Emmeline's death? Was his disappearance an admission of guilt? Or was he perhaps a victim? Had he seen something? Did he know something? Was his life in danger? Was he even still alive?

It was only when I turned to look for Uncle Albert that I noticed that James had been sitting in a lounger, quite close to us. He wore a scowl, which was becoming something of his custom of late. And if I didn't know better, I would have said that he had been listening in on my conversation with Poppy.

CHAPTER 15

As we made our way down after a day of fruitless birdwatching, it was clear to me that taking charge of directing Monte Verita had completely driven Nicholas out of Poppy's head. According to Poppy, he had been keeping to his hut, drinking, and generally avoiding any contact with the other residents. She had gone off him.

And it was a good thing. Because as we were making our way down, a donkey cart carrying several policemen passed us going in the opposite direction. I even exchanged a grudging nod with the senior policeman from the ball. Since the road led to only one place, I had no doubt he was on his way to Monte Verita.

I wanted to jump out of our own donkey cart and follow the police back to Monte Verita, but on second thought, I decided against it. Poppy was perfectly placed to transmit all that was about to transpire in the community.

But I had forgotten that Monte Verita had no telephone, and I now sat dejected in my room at the Grand Hotel, devoid of news. Worse still, I knew the hotel was buzzing with news, but I had no way of learning what it was.

All I knew was that a journalist from the local press, hungry for news, had treated a policeman to a few drinks at the hotel bar. Within the hour, by way of the barman, anyone at the hotel with a valet or a lady's maid worth their salt knew the intricacies of the police investigation. For the first time since leaving England, I regretted choosing to be a modern woman and not having a maid travel with me. She would have been indispensable at this moment. And she probably would have done a better job at conjuring up fairy wings for the ball, I had to admit.

Just then, a soft knock at the door drew me out of my thoughts.

It was Wilford, my uncle's valet. He had come all the way from the villa, on instructions from my uncle, to bring me a book on Alpine rodents. My uncle had insisted it was most educational, and I might be interested in perusing it this evening. I shrugged and took the book from him.

As he was about to depart, he turned and said, "Lady Caroline, I wonder if you have heard the latest developments in the Miss Emmeline Walpole-Semperton's case?"

My heart made a happy leap. I knew Wilford was one of the most capable valets around, and I had no doubt that, despite his brief stay in Locarno, he had already established an information network with the other valets in town. "Have there been any developments?" I asked, feigning ignorance on the matter.

"It appears Mr. Nicholas Bradley has been arrested for the murder of Miss Walpole-Semperton," he said, without displaying any undue sentiment.

"Has he?" I said, my voice betraying my elation at finally getting a hold of the rumor circulating the hotel. "And what was his motive?" I asked in a more measured tone.

"The police suspect that there has been some unpleasantness involving what I believe is known as a lovers' triangle, My Lady," he said, casting his eyes down modestly.

"Really?" Although I had suspected something similar, I was more than curious to find out the thoughts of the police on the matter.

"That's right, My Lady. It appears that while residing at Monte Verita, Mr. Bradley developed an unhealthy obsession with Miss Walpole-Semperton. I also understand that the young lady was from a very wealthy family, so the police are exploring financial gain as a motive as well."

"But what about the person Miss Walpole-Semperton had seen at the party? The one that she had been afraid of?" I asked. While I had also suspected Nicholas myself, I thought the mysterious figure at the party should not be overlooked. Plus, if my hunch was right, the mysterious reflection had pinched Poppy's camera.

"The police suspect that Mr. Bradley fabricated

that part of the story in order to throw the police off his scent."

I was about to protest and tell Wilford that I had overheard Emmeline herself speak of seeing someone at the party, but decided to keep that bit of information to myself for the present. Then again, it might have been Nicholas himself, in disguise, who had frightened Emmeline.

"Furthermore," the valet continued, "it appears that they now suspect Mr. Bradley of having contributed to Mr. Spencer Grafton's drowning."

"Really!?" I exclaimed.

He nodded. "I believe you were present during that particular accident?" he asked delicately. I nodded in turn. "The police now think the drowning was not accidental."

"What evidence do they have?" I said, barely able to contain my excitement.

"It is pure conjecture on their part. I believe they are looking to get a confession out of the young gentleman on that account. But they believe that after Mr. Bradley stopped the boat and Mr. Grafton fell off his skis, Mr. Bradley held the other gentleman down under water until he drowned. Furthermore, when the police went to retrieve the motorboat, abandoned on the lake after the accident, they had no trouble starting the motor. They believe Mr. Bradley only pretended that the motor had stalled."

"How interesting," I said. Flashes of the

drowning came back to me. I watched in my mind's eye as Nicholas leaned out of the boat over Spencer. From where we were standing, it had appeared as though Nicholas was trying to help Spencer into the boat. But looked at a different way, he could have been pushing him down and using all his might to prevent him from getting on the boat. Could Nicholas have drowned Spencer? The police appeared to think so. "But what about the body?" I said at last.

"The police are convinced that it will turn up soon enough. The lake is notorious for underwater currents and unexpected whirlpools. But bodies usually wash up on the shore in the end. Though there have been a few cases where the bodies were never recovered. The villages all along the lake and the few islands have been informed to be on the lookout for a body. Even the ones in Italy."

I thanked Wilford for the book and the information, and he departed.

As my mind raced over the details of the latest developments, I confess they stirred up some uneasiness in me. I'd also suspected that Nicholas was involved in Emmeline's murder, but now that the police had arrested him, I wasn't so certain.

For one, what was his motive? What did he have to gain by her death?

I could understand why he would want to remove Spencer as a rival, but once he had achieved that by drowning him, why would he turn on Emmeline?

Had Emmeline suspected that Nicholas had killed Spencer? I thought back to her reaction at the beach. At first she had seemed really distraught, but then her distress had turned to anger, and she had left abruptly, as though she blamed Nicholas for Spencer's death.

Had she threatened Nicholas that she would reveal her suspicions to the police? Was that why he had strangled her?

But that did not explain the mysterious figure Emmeline had seen at the party. One explanation would be that it had been Nicholas playing tricks on her. But she had also seen the figure before the ball, at Monte Verita. Who was that person and why were they following her around?

Emmeline's father was presumably in South America. What if he'd come back? But why would she be frightened of him? And why would he kill her?

By all accounts, there was a large fortune attached to Emmeline. I shivered. As a wealthy woman myself, I had never considered the possibility that someone might murder me for my money. I pushed those thoughts aside and brought my mind back to the problem at hand.

What about the disturbances at Monte Verita the police had referred to? Poppy had also hinted at animosity between the locals and the residents at Monte Verita. Had Emmeline been engaged in something untoward? Something that had scandalized the locals, something that had driven one of them to murder her?

I sighed. I did not have enough information to go on. I needed to learn more about Emmeline.

CHAPTER 16

The next morning, just as I was preparing to leave the hotel to join my uncle at the villa for a day of secretarial toil, out of the corner of my eye, I caught a glimpse of a messenger boy in red livery angling for me. In his hand, he held a note.

The note bore an uncomfortable resemblance to something my mother would send, and I was determined to evade him. But the plucky young man seemed just as determined to deliver it to me. He chased me down the corridors, and just as I was about to slip out into the gardens, I made the amateurish mistake of turning to check behind me. Satisfied with the superiority of my skills, and convinced that I had outsmarted him, I turned around just in time to see him pop up right in front of me.

I had to concede that he knew the hotel's shortcuts better than me and accepted the letter grudgingly. But I tipped him generously for a game well played.

On second thought, it was perhaps my generosity which inspired such pluck and determination in these young hotel types.

It was with a trembling hand that I opened the

telegram from my mother. It felt lighter in my palm than her usual missives. I tried to think what could have elicited a communication from her. Perhaps she had identified a suitable mate for me among the residents of Monte Verita? Perhaps she was under the mistaken impression, like my uncle, that it was full of pious young men?

A renegade thought flashed through my mind, and I cast a glance around surreptitiously. Had Lady Morton, a matron of biblical proportions and dread, managed to track me down? Had she corresponded with my mother yet again? Was I to be united with her Cecil after all?

But a happy jolt swept through my body as I uncorked the note. It was from my chum in London, Elanor, whom I had met at typing school.

One of the chief reasons why I had been dispatched to my uncle, in addition to proving too fastidious about my marriage prospects (according to my mother), was that I had attended a typing school in London as part of a jolly good scavenger hunt that had gone on for a few weeks. Upon learning about my stint at the school, my mother declared that I had ruined my chances with said marriage prospects, and had thus sent me to Uncle Albert.

Elanor, who now worked for Lloyd's in London, the insurance chaps, had sent me a rather long note in which she explained that she and my other typing school chums had read about Emmeline's death in the newspapers. Realizing that I was in the same city as the victim, and in anticipation of a cable from me, they had decided to preempt me, and had dug up information about Emmeline before I could even ask for it.

A warm feeling of gratitude spread through me. *Hurrah for ambitious young women in typing schools!*

Elanor had discovered a life insurance policy in Emmeline Walpole-Semperton's name at Lloyd's and had imparted the gist of its contents in the telegram.

I stopped reading. I needed to find a quiet place to think. A small sofa in one corner, hidden by a potted fern, presented the perfect place to read in peace.

I returned to the telegram. The beneficiary clause of the life insurance document was rather curious. In fact, the clause contained two curious points. The first was that in the event of Emmeline's death, the money from her life insurance would go to her husband. And the second—that her husband was the dead Spencer Grafton.

The news was quite unexpected. I looked up from the telegram and let my eyes roam over the intricate gilding of the hotel's walls. Nothing in Emmeline's behavior towards Spencer had hinted that they were married. I wondered if anyone at Monte Verita knew about the marriage. I wondered if Nicholas knew about it.

This new piece of information made Emmeline's appearance at the Midsummer ball even more peculiar. Why would a grieving widow go to a costume ball the day after her husband's death?

Or was she perhaps *not* a grieving widow? Why had they kept their marriage secret? Were they perhaps in the process of getting a divorce?

I needed to find out more about Emmeline and Spencer, but first I needed to finish reading the telegram.

Elanor went on to say that Spencer had a life insurance with Lloyd's as well, and his policy benefited Emmeline. But even if Emmeline had lived, Elanor went on to clarify, his policy would not have been paid out to Emmeline because his body had not been found.

I put the telegram in my lap. Questions swirled in my mind. How did insurance policies work? Would they be paid out to someone else now that both Spencer and Emmeline were dead? I didn't know the answer.

And what about a will? It was worth checking to see if Nicholas perhaps was a beneficiary of Emmeline's.

The question of wills reminded me of Emmeline's fortune. Where did that fit in? To whom did her money now go?

A pesky thought of her failed industrial father kept springing to mind. Could he be behind all this, after all?

I went in search of a messenger boy. I needed to send several telegrams to London.

Over the next two days, I established a steady correspondence with my chums in London and began to form an impression of Emmeline and her family.

As mortified as my mother had been to discover that I had participated in a typing class in London, she had been additionally horrified to learn that I had become friends with girls whose parents were in trade.

But my mother was as resourceful as she was snobbish and had bullied her friends and acquaintances in placing the girls from my typing class at various venerable British institutions. Thus, in addition to Lloyd's, I now had friends at the War Office (Jane), the Church of England (Louisa), and the Bank of England (Philippa). And they were perfectly placed to provide me with information no one else could.

With the help of my friends, a picture began to emerge about Emmeline. And the picture was not what I had expected.

Using her contacts at the Bank of England, Philippa was able to shed light on the business dealings of Emmeline's father and uncle. This information was supplemented by war contracts the two industrialists had with the War Office, supplied by Jane. And Elanor was able to elucidate this further by supplying information about a series of insurance payouts to various victims of several industrial accidents at various enterprises belonging to Emmeline's family.

Even Louisa, installed at the Church of England by my mother, contributed in her way. Bemoaning that she rarely had much to contribute to my investigations, she had taken it upon herself to review old newspapers for articles about the Walpole-Semperton family.

At the heart of the Walpole-Semperton family's history was the fact that Emmeline's father and uncle had been quite unlucky in business. Despite their contracts and machinations, a series of industrial accidents had ruined them. The courts had awarded sums to the families of the victims and the government had canceled any further contracts.

All of this brought on the sudden and rather surprising cognizance that Emmeline had in fact been penniless upon her death. Any money that had remained in the family after her father's failed business affairs had gone to her brother, and her radical way of living had ensured that she was disowned by her family. All she had to her name was her insurance policy.

Furthermore, the family had not approved of

the marriage between Emmeline and Spencer. From various pieces of gossip procured during a fruitful trip to the area where the Walpole-Sempertons lived, Louisa had discovered that although Spencer hailed from a respectable and aristocratic family, the Walpole-Sempertons did not approve of him. He had been penniless. And though Emmeline's father had offered Spencer a job at one of his few going concerns, Spencer had not accepted. Like Emmeline, he preferred to travel and attend parties.

According to the local newspapers, the newly married couple had discovered that by professing radical ideas, they could make their way across Europe, visiting various disillusioned wealthy people and living off their generosity. The newspapers professed that there was a whole network of radical thinkers, writers and artists who lived off their shocking ideas, lecturing others about the evils of idle wealth, while never lifting a finger to do an honest day's work themselves.

I put the telegrams aside. I had assumed that Emmeline's death was somehow connected to her wealth. So where did that leave me now? If it was not money, what possible motive could anyone have to kill her?

CHAPTER 17

One of the grander meeting rooms at the Grand Hotel Locarno had undergone extensive renovation in preparation for something tedious, such as a high-level meeting of heads of state at the end of the year. Though what could be so important as to encroach on the festive season, I could not think.

Sensitive as hotel managers were to the intricacies of the British peerage, the present one, a certain Herr Schmid, agreed, somewhat reluctantly—and not until the mention of my mother's name—to let me use the meeting room as my own communications center. I'd grown tired of playing hide and seek in the hotel lobby with the messenger boys, especially because I somehow always tended to lose.

In addition to the meeting room, I had at my disposal a telephone connected to the hotel's switchboard, which in a few minutes, and going through the exchanges of several countries, would connect me to London.

Thus settled in my new office, I commenced a daily correspondence with London.

Familiar with my methods of investigation by

now, my friends had taken it upon themselves to look up every mortal soul that the newspapers in London had mentioned in connection with Emmeline's death. And the name that had stood out front and center from the pages of the rags was Nicholas Bradley.

Trouble was, Nicholas Bradley did not figure in any of the records my chums looked up. They concluded that Nicholas Bradley was either such a dull chap that both the government and the church had simply failed to take notice of him— and I, for one, knew him to be anything but dull— or there was something more intriguing going on. For a moment, my chums were stumped. But this dead end did not stop them and they continued to dig through the profusion of paperwork that is the hallmark of a well-run bureaucracy.

Then, the most interesting news arrived by way of Louisa. And it was a corker. According to Louisa, Nicholas Bradley was not a real person. Put simply, a chap named Nicholas Bradley did not exist.

But Louisa was not as cruel as to leave it at that. She had uncovered the missing clue.

Having a taste in books which ran to those with dense social commentary, with a penchant for plays written in the Socratic method, Louisa recognized the name. A little more digging let her discover that Nicholas Bradley was a *nom de plume*.

So who was hiding behind the name Nicholas Bradley?

It was only thanks to some additional sleuthing during her lunch breaks and the assistance of a sympathetic reference library clerk at the British Library, who also happened to have connections at one of London's more experimental publishing houses, that Louisa had eked out a name—Nicholas Spaulding.

Having secured the real name behind the pseudonym, Louisa had easily discovered a link between Nicholas Spaulding and the Walpole-Semperton family. To complete the picture, Elanor at Lloyd's had stepped in.

From the insurer's records, Elanor was able to retrieve a list of settlements made by Emmeline's father to families of victims of industrial accidents at his factories. One of these families was the Spaulding family.

I tore my eyes away from the telegram to collect my thoughts. This information certainly placed recent events in a new perspective. If Nicholas' father or some other close family member had died in an industrial accident brought on by negligence on the part of management, it would give Nicholas a powerful motive for murder.

But why Emmeline?

As the Walpole-Semperton father seemed to be hiding out somewhere in South America, Nicholas might have looked upon Emmeline as the next most just target. Sins of the father and all that. This was not a lovers' triangle or a random impulse brought on by bohemian excess, which was a motive I'd heard the police were currently leaning towards. This was retribution for past wrongs.

I needed to speak to Nicholas. But he was in jail. It was time to employ the far-reaching connections and influence of my family's name.

The British aristocracy was like a giant spider web, I'd always thought. Regardless of how large it grew and how many spokes and threads were added, all the families remained interconnected. Tugging on the web at one end usually could get one a response at quite another spot on the web.

It was with this knowledge that I approached Uncle Albert. At first I'd thought of seeking out my mother's help—she would undoubtedly know whom to tug on to get immediate results. But I preferred not to disturb her. Like a black widow spider, it was best not to get tangled in her web.

"Uncle Albert," I addressed the aging relation, while perusing his correspondence, "I'm faced with a bit of a difficulty."

My uncle shifted uncomfortably in his seat. "Does it have to do with a young man?" he asked timidly.

I marveled at his uncanny perceptiveness. "In a manner of speaking, yes. You see, there is a young man in jail—"

But something about the dejected manner in which the red fez hung on my uncle's head told me he'd got the wrong end of the stick.

"It's nothing like that, uncle!" I protested. I saw now that I needed to be more direct. "Do we know someone at the British Consulate here?"

My uncle's eyes widened. "Is it as serious as that?" my uncle asked with a gasp. "No matter," he said, recovering himself and stiffening his back. His eyes were now darting from side to side. "I'm sure the boy's family could be paid off, and the boy shipped off as an envoy extraordinary to Uruguay or somewhere…" He prattled on about all the obscure government positions in remote geographical places where an unworthy young man could be concealed, away from society's prying eyes.

I sighed and paused to think of a different approach. I gave it another go. "The man in this case has done nothing wrong…well, not to me anyway," I began, but I could sense that I was getting just as muddled as my uncle. "Let me begin again. I'm trying to establish whether we have any connections—"

"Pardon the interruption, My Lady," Wilford intervened. "But I think I can be of assistance." I nodded my consent. "I believe what Lady Caroline is asking, My Lord," he turned to Uncle Albert, "is whether you have any connections with the British Diplomatic Mission in Switzerland that could be used to put pressure on the local authorities and help Lady Caroline secure an audience with the young man currently sequestered in the Locarno jail for the murder of Miss Walpole-Semperton."

I nodded enthusiastically and held my breath to see if Wilford had done the trick.

"By Jove, Young Carol," my uncle cried out, "why didn't you say so?" He clapped his hands, and color returned to his cheeks. "Right, ho! Our family is as well represented in the ranks of the British Diplomatic Service as any other. Better than even Lord Fetherly's, I'd say. I'm sure we can worm a relation out of the woodwork, as it were. Now, Wilford," he turned to his trusted valet, "help me think."

"Well, My Lord, there is Lord Bramblebee's nephew who married Lady Priscilla—"

My uncle shook his head. "No, you are thinking of George's boy," my uncle corrected him. "He is the Oriental Secretary at Constantinople."

"I believe you are correct, My Lord," Wilford conceded.

"What about Archibald, Reginald's sister's younger boy?" my uncle ventured.

"If my memory serves me right, My Lord, he's the cultural attache in Berlin."

"So he is," my uncle agreed, somewhat disappointed. I could see by the strain on his face that his mind was jumping from branch to branch on our gnarled family tree, trying to latch on to the right one. "What about Lord Spencer's boy, Gerald?"

The valet shook his head. "He's the envoy to the Grand Duchy of Luxembourg, My Lord."

"We're getting closer, at any rate," my uncle said with a twinkle in his eyes. I could tell he found the exercise invigorating. "What about Lord Pickletrop's grandson by his daughter's second marriage to Sir Basil Stelton?" came my uncle's next suggestion.

"Ah, if you remember, My Lord," Wilford began in a solemn voice, "he was involved in the Oslo Affair, and was dispatched to Bogota, in Colombia."

"So he was. So he was," my uncle said merrily. "The Oslo Affair was a display of remarkable ineptitude even by the standards of the Foreign Office. Sheer poetry." He stared longingly in the distance for a few moments. "Now, let's see... where were we?"

"Looking for a diplomatic connection in Switzerland, My Lord," Wilford reminded him.

"Oh, yes...I say! What about my cousin, Sir Percy Dewhurst? His wife's first cousin, a Lady Gwendolyn, married someone with a position at Whitehall—"

"Sir Rupert Overton, My Lord?" suggested Wilford.

"That's right. Now, didn't he have a brother who

at one time was married to one of the Rycroft sisters?"

"That's right, My Lord. Daphne Rycroft."

"If memory serves me right,"—that was always a hazard with Uncle Albert, I mused—"her second boy from her fourth marriage, to Sir Edmund Kettlewell...I think the boy is now the British plenipotentiary in Bern," my uncle said with triumph in his voice.

"I believe you are correct, My Lord," Wilford replied, and inclined his head as though recognizing my uncle's superior knowledge of labyrinthine relations. "I will dispatch a messenger boy to arrange a call to the British Mission right away, My Lord."

My uncle's genealogical arithmetics was a performance worthy of a standing ovation. I was well aware that I'd been granted a rare glimpse at Uncle Albert's bygone brilliance. Though one had heard rumors that my uncle's sharp mind had been the foundation upon which he had built a successful career, which had stretched across the far reaches of the empire, I'd always had my doubts.

I skipped across the room and gave him a peck on the cheek.

He looked up at me with misty eyes. "By the by, Bogota is another good place for that fellow of yours that's giving you trouble, Caroline," he said, and tapped the side of his nose.

CHAPTER 18

As impressive as Uncle Albert's connections with the diplomatic missions across Europe were, in the end, they fell short of producing the desired result.

Several telegrams and phone calls to the Locarno police station from increasingly higher-ranking Swiss officials failed to secure a passage for me to Nicholas' cell. My uncle's relation in Bern suggested that the defeat was likely due to an ongoing animosity between Switzerland's Italian-speaking south, and the country's German-speaking north.

Thus, the local police did not feel obliged to consent to the requests sent to them by the ruling powers in Bern. In fact, they delighted in the obstruction.

Another way in had to be found.

Relief came from an unlikely source—Poppy. Born into a family of highly decorated military men, Poppy was well aware of the adage, attributed to Napoleon, that an army marches on its stomach. Perceiving my problem, she had no doubt the same axiom applied to policemen lazing behind desks.

Thanks to her ambitious reconstructive programme at Monte Verita, Poppy had quickly formed close connections with local tradesmen and producers. And one of the closest was with the baker in the village of Ascona, who, as the aunt of one of the policemen in Locarno, knew of the institution's weakness for a cake called *Torta di Pane*.

It was a slice of this freshly baked cake—made with cocoa, filled with dried fruits, raisins, ground almonds, topped with a layer of pine nuts, and all soaked in a generous amount of grappa—that the Locarno policeman on duty was now tucking into.

And I was sitting happily in Nicholas' jail cell.

Expecting Nicholas to be racked with guilt and loathing his current predicament, I was surprised to find him in rude health. The luster in his hair was back, as was the twinkle in his velvet eyes. Sitting on his cot, he lounged quite nonchalantly against the bare stone wall of his cell. In short, he displayed a devil-may-care attitude, emphasized by his rolled-up shirtsleeves.

He also didn't seem disturbed when I confronted him about his true identity. But he objected most vehemently at the suggestion that he had employed a false name to deceive Emmeline.

He pushed a hand through his thick hair. "Yes, I admit that my first impulse was to despise her for the sorrow her family's greed had brought on my family. I lost my father and older brother during an explosion at a munitions factory owned by her family. But it all changed when I met her."

"Then why use an alias if not for deception?" I asked.

He smiled. "It's my pen-name. I'm a writer," he clarified, as though I were a simpleton. "I wrote a series of interpretivist treatises on the transcendental socio-economic plight of the progressive proletariat, analyzed through the prism of humanistic anthroposophy."

I met him with a blank stare. Although I recognized some of the words—especially *anthroposophy*, which I'd picked up recently from Poppy—strung together, the words made little sense.

He shook his head derisively at my obtuseness. "My work explores the thesis that a clear understanding of the spiritual world can free the individual from the oppression of external authority," he explained.

Still nothing.

He pressed on, undeterred. "The volumes were quite successful," he said, and I wondered how anyone could penetrate beyond the title of these treatises, but kept that observation to myself. "My work was compared to the work of John Locke and David Hume. Others hailed the volumes as a modern interpretation of philosophical empiricism and skepticism." I got the impression that he was boasting, although I couldn't understand why. "Given the success of my books among the intelligentsia of Europe, I chose to continue using my pen-name, under which I'm best known in those circles. There was no malice behind it." He leaned back with satisfaction. But my mind was quite muddled as I tried to make sense of what he'd said.

Then his countenance changed, and a shadow of sorrow flashed across his face. "Upon meeting Emmeline," he said, his tone almost regretful, "I formed a deep spiritual bond with her. She, as the daughter of an industrialist, had an innate understanding of the philosophical implications of destructive rationalism and the imperialistic roots of transcendental idealism in sustaining the feudalistic system of modern industrialism."

Having attended university, I could ruminate about logical positivism with the best of them, and construct simple Latin ditties to rival those of any Etonian schoolboy. But I could feel myself slipping slowly into a coma, my brain numbed by the impenetrable philosophical ramblings of Nicholas.

As he droned on, the last vestiges of reason in my brain began to protest that Nicholas' verbal shenanigans might well be a ploy to keep me from getting to the real point of my visit.

I shook my head, as though waking from a dream. Nicholas' soliloquy reminded me painfully of a conversation I'd had with Lilibeth Galardsel.

Lilibeth Galardsel had been a vivacious debutante two years ago. Having become engaged to the writer and notable playwright Hugh Frances, she had taken up an unnatural interest in modern literature. Just before I had escaped from London, she had inebriated me over afternoon tea with a disquisition on the semiotic parallels of the narrative allegory between James Joyce's *Ulysses* and John Bunyan's *A Pilgrim's Progress*.

In Lilibeth's case, the literary discussion was designed to distract me from the fact that I had come to collect a rather exquisite sapphire tiara I had lent her for a ball the previous season that she had failed to return. I now wondered if Nicholas was using the same trick to distract me from the real reason for my visit—namely, his involvement in Emmeline's death.

I needed to regain control of the conversation, so I decided to use the tactic of surprise. "Did you know that Spencer and Emmeline were married?"

If Nicholas was surprised by my question, he didn't show it.

"I knew," he said. He smiled and the look on his face gave me to understand that he was above the constraints of such bourgeois institutions.

I was not about to cower under his gaze. "Was there a romantic relationship between you and Emmeline?"

"What if there was?" he asked and leaned forward on his elbows, a glint of mischief in his eyes. I became acutely aware of the muscles straining under his shirtsleeves. And yet, as I examined him more closely, I decided that there was something quite hypocritical about him. Why did he live in a community supported by the benefactions of heiresses and the idle rich? Why was he not on the barricades with proletariats throwing bricks at industrialists instead of attending balls given by them?

But before I could ask, the policeman on duty came to tell us that he had finished with his cake and I only had a few more minutes before his supervisor would be back and I would have to leave.

Although, perhaps, he didn't actually mention the cake.

I scrambled through the questions in my head. Which ones were the most important to ask? I admonished myself for allowing Nicholas to prattle on about his books and ideas.

"Did Emmeline know that your father and brother had died in an accident at one of her father's factories?"

He allowed the slightest spasm to cross his face, but did not reply. His eyes examined my face for a few moments. Although his gaze was intoxicating, I was not about to be thwarted. Plus, I was running short on time. "Was there a lovers' triangle between you and Spencer and Emmeline?"

He smiled again, as though he was enjoying

talking about all this. "There was. She had married Spencer when they were very young. He was brawny and a good rugby player. I guess she found such things attractive once. But he had rather unsophisticated ideas about the world, and she now craved intellect." I assumed he was referring to his intellect. "Spencer was unhappy about living at Monte Verita," he continued. "He felt out of place. But he remained, because Emmeline loved it. She thrived in the freedom of the community."

His rendition sounded truthful. But I wanted to know more about him. "And what about you? What led you to Monte Verita? Had you followed Emmeline there?"

He shook his head. "It happened quite by chance, though given our mutual interests, our souls would have guided us to each other sooner rather than later. As it was, I was visiting one of the residents to develop my ideas on anthroposophy when I met Emmeline."

"When did you find out who she was?"

"Oh, I knew right away. With a family name like that, it's hard not to know who she was."

A thought flashed through my mind. I had overlooked something. "But why did she not use Spencer's family name?"

Nicholas laughed at my naivete. "She wasn't his property," he said.

"So you never told her that her father was responsible for your family's loss?"

"I planned to, at first. I had nothing to hide or be ashamed of. But she was such a gentle creature. So otherworldly, somehow. I didn't have the heart to tell her."

"Do you think Spencer knew who you really were?"

"Why should he? I had never told anyone. Plus, it was not important. The hatred I carried for her family died in my breast when I met her."

"Did Spencer suspect that you were in love with Emmeline?"

"I didn't hide my feelings," Nicholas said with a shrug.

"And did Emmeline return your affections?"

"She didn't hide them either."

"And did Spencer not mind?" I asked, trying to hide my incredulity.

Nicholas did not reply right away. He adopted the countenance of a spiritual leader, attempting to explain his sophisticated ideas to the uninitiated. "Monte Verita is a different place," he pontificated. "It functions outside the realm of the impediments put on the individual by a bourgeois society. It's a place to be free."

By now I was accustomed to his tricks of evading answering my questions, and simply went on to the next question I had in mind. "If Emmeline was in love with you, did she ever think of leaving Spencer?"

"We had discussed it."

"How would Spencer have reacted?"

"He would have done anything for Emmeline. He would have let her go eventually, once he understood that it was her wish to be with me."

I wondered if Nicholas was right. I knew little about Spencer, but from what I had seen at Monte Verita, he appeared to be deeply in love with Emmeline. But would that have made him more likely to want her to be happy and let her go? Or would it have made him fight for her?

But was there someone else in this relationship? My thoughts drifted to Brother Gregor. What was his role in this complicated affair?

"Could you think of anyone who would have wanted Emmeline dead?"

Nicholas' eyes darkened. "No."

"What about the person she saw at the ball?" I pressed.

"It was just her imagination. There was no one there," he said firmly.

And yet, I thought, someone was there. And killed her.

"We'd started planning a future together," Nicholas interrupted my thoughts. "We talked about publishing more books, spreading my ideas all over Europe. Opening schools for the proletariat to educate them about the power of spiritual freedom."

"And how were you going to support all of that?" I asked. Despite how successful Nicholas purported his books were, I doubted they provided him with much income.

Nicholas cocked an eyebrow. "Emmeline was an heiress," he said simply.

I flinched. Did Nicholas not know that Emmeline had no fortune of her own? But I decided to keep that news to myself.

Perhaps realizing for the first time that Emmeline's death had deprived him of capital for his venture, Nicholas attempted to interest me in some of his other ideas. But I'd had enough of that and as the policeman came to usher me out, I took my leave most willingly.

As I left the police station, I was still uncertain about what to make of Nicholas.

On the one hand, he seemed to have been quite enamored with Emmeline and I doubted that he would kill her, not least because he believed she could finance his dreams.

On the other hand, there was something of the charlatan about him. All his looks and smiles seemed to be calculated to charm and disarm.

Was he a snake-oil salesman of radical ideas? His books struck me as gibberish, full of random outlandish terms and ideas which the intelligentsia probably only purported to understand out of conceit.

And I continued to believe that he was hiding the identity of the person Emmeline had seen at the ball. But why?

It was only then that I remembered that I had forgotten to ask him about Brother Gregor, but the prospect of spending more time with Nicholas meant that I would have to find the answer to that particular question in a different manner.

Riding on the tram back to the hotel, a dark thought surfaced in my mind. If Nicholas had not known about Emmeline's lack of fortune, could the police be right that something more sinister had occurred on the lake that day? Had Nicholas failed to help Spencer while he was drowning? Had Spencer's drowning not been an accident? Had Nicholas pushed his rival under the water?

But even if that threw some light on Spencer's demise, what had led to Emmeline's?

CHAPTER 19

The meeting with Nicholas had left me strangely restless and unsatisfied. I was certain he was hiding something, but I didn't know what.

I had reviewed our conversation and stripping it of its flourishes, I had pared it down to this: there was indeed a lovers' triangle between Emmeline, Spencer and Nicholas. Emmeline and Nicholas had formed a connection over his radical ideas, and Emmeline had offered to use her fortune to further his ambitions. Trouble was, Emmeline did not have a fortune. Had she lied to Nicholas or was Nicholas lying to me?

And where did Spencer fit in? Would he have given up Emmeline as easily as Nicholas had suggested? Had Nicholas taken matters into his own hands, so to speak, and drowned Spencer? Had he then killed Emmeline at the party? But to what end?

Why had Emmeline claimed to have seen someone at the party? And why was Nicholas denying it?

An idea streaked through my mind. What if Nicholas and this mysterious person were conspiring? Who could that person be? The missing Brother Gregor? Or...

Another idea popped up in my mind. I looked around my uncle's room, where I was going over his correspondence of the day, as though seeing it for the first time. It was as though the proverbial scales fell off my eyes.

Why had I not considered Mr. Linnaeus as a suspect? The invitation to his party, the out of the way passageway where Emmeline was found, the arbitrary placement of the electric fan, the vague reference to a business relationship between Mr. Linnaeus and Emmeline's father, even Mr. Linnaeus' inexplicable correspondence with residents at Monte Verita, all seemed to be quite suggestive.

"Uncle," I turned to him, "what do you know about Mr. Linnaeus?"

"Oh, many things," he said and placed his book down, a wistful look in his eyes. "He was a great scientist. A noted zoologist and botanist who formalized the binomial nomenclature for all living things. If you are interested, I have a wonderful collection of four volumes on the life and work of the noted Swede—"

"No, not Carl Linnaeus," I said, trying to keep frustration out of my voice. "Mr. Mikael Linnaeus, your current host."

"Oh, him," my uncle said and clammed up. "I know he's not a descendent of Carl Linnaeus."

"Yes. But even so. Don't you know anything

more about him? After all, he is a member of the Royal Society."

"Well," my uncle said and sighed. "There are some among us who think he should be excommunicated. But the majority have had their heads turned by him and will not hear of it."

Now we were getting somewhere. I was sure my uncle knew something damning about Mr. Linnaeus.

"What is your objection to Mr. Linnaeus?" I asked.

"Well, for one, he cannot name a single mosquito species found in Sweden. And there are forty-seven species at last count. The floodwater mosquito, *Aedes sticticus*, should easily come to anyone's mind." My uncle sighed and shook his head, the fez threatening to fall off. "I find his company tedious, with little to talk about."

I wondered how to proceed from here, but my uncle continued. "But there are some among the members, who shall remain unnamed, that have voted to have the man remain in our midst because they discovered an exquisite specimen of *Cerambyx cerdo*, a great Capricorn beetle, on his estate. The beetle is sadly extinct on the British Isles, and the more unscrupulous among the members of the Royal Society see a continued alliance with Mr. Linnaeus as an opportunity to augment their beetle collections."

I realized speaking to my uncle about anything

outside the scope of the Royal Society was a lost cause, but I was determined to give it another try. "But what about his business? Do you know anything about his business?"

"Caroline!" Uncle Albert exclaimed. "What society do you think we are running here? One doesn't discuss business at the Royal Society meetings!" I could see my uncle was outraged. I had rarely seen him so shaken up. "This is not a guild of saddle makers. It's the Royal Society for Natural History Appreciation. We didn't get a royal charter to discuss money."

Regretting that I had brought up the topic at all, I turned around in my seat and attempted to focus on the letters spread out in front of me on the desk.

"But now that you mention it," my uncle's voice floated up through the silence unexpectedly, "there was some discussion of Mr. Linnaeus' background at one point. I just can't remember exactly what."

I swiveled around in my chair but had to wait a few minutes for him to fully recollect the events. In the meantime, I wondered how much Wilford knew, and whether he could contribute something of value to the conversation.

"I got it!" my uncle exclaimed. "He had invented a way for preserving food—pinched the method from a French cookbook, rather—and tried to patent it. But at the same time, an Englishmen was patenting the same method, stolen from the same book by the same French cook. They got into some sort of argument about patents, and both rushed to patent the method in America. I'm not sure who won at the time. But later, the Englishman got into a spot of bother and some people died. He went bankrupt. By the looks of it, Mr. Linnaeus prospered." He paused, and by the strain in his eyes, I could tell there was something more he was endeavoring to recall, so I didn't interrupt him. "He mentioned to some of the members that he is working on a new prototype. Something very secret that he is trying to find a buyer for."

"What sort of thing?" I asked.

"Oh, I can't remember. Something war related. Some gun or other. Or an engine. Or perhaps it was a new way of canning food. It had something to do with metal, in any case," he waved off the details as irrelevant.

Although I would have to confirm it, I had no doubt in my mind that the Englishman my uncle had referred to was Emmeline Walpole-Semperton's father. The facts corresponded. And Mr. Linnaeus himself had admitted to knowing Emmeline's father.

Was Mr. Linnaeus responsible for Emmeline's death? After all, her body was found in a part of the house that led to his office.

But what would his motive be? I dismissed the idea that he had killed her as a retribution of sorts as an outlandish theory. But what about this new invention my uncle mentioned? What if Emmeline had been working with her father to steal Mr. Linnaeus' new invention? Had he caught her sneaking around his office?

CHAPTER 20

Opportunity to speak with Mr. Linnaeus came during tea time. Despite what my uncle had said, I found him to be an engaging and well-educated man, even if he was not familiar with all forty-seven species of mosquitoes in Sweden.

"Were you surprised to see Emmeline at your party the other night?" I ventured.

"Why should I? I invited her," he said, taking a sip of tea.

"But surely you knew about the drowning," I said. "It was my understanding that we had used your boat that day? Did you not think it strange that she came to the party after that young man drowned?"

"No more than you," he said with a small smile, alluding to the fact I had been present at the drowning as well. "Perhaps she did not know the young man who drowned well?" he suggested.

"I have reason to believe he was her husband," I said in a measured tone, scrutinizing his reaction.

He looked at me for a moment before answering. "But that is most surprising. Why would she have come to a party?"

"Why, indeed," I said and nodded. "I understand you knew Miss Emmeline Walpole-Semperton's father."

He nodded.

"Were you in the same line of business?" I asked.

"I was," he said, but he did not elaborate.

"What do you think could have enticed Emmeline to visit the part of the house where she was found?" I asked casually.

"I could not say," he replied.

"Forgive me for being forward, but I heard that her father and you were something of business rivals," I said, and then regretted my impertinence. My lack of progress was getting the better of me.

Mr. Linnaeus, however, did not seem offended. "That is not a secret," he said. "I believe it is well known that he stole an improved formula for the preservation of meat rations from me and tried to patent it in America. We were partners before he tried to cheat me. And I consider myself lucky to have escaped from his partnership, given all the problems his business ran into later on."

Mr. Linnaeus struck me as an honest man, and I decided to run my theory past him. "I have a little theory, and I wonder what you might think of it. Were you working on some new invention or a business idea?" I said.

"Yes, I was. How did you know?" he asked, a hint of suspicion in his eyes.

"Just a hunch," I said enigmatically. "Do you think Emmeline had come to the house in order to steal it?"

"I hope not," he said. "The formula is locked up in my safe...." he trailed off and a deep furrow formed on his brow. I was sure he had never considered this possibility. Did that make him innocent of Emmeline's death? "I can assure you that the safe has not been broken into," he said. "I'm confident the young woman's death had nothing to do with my business dealings."

We sat in companionable silence, sipping our tea, each lost in thought under the wisteria-covered pergola in Mr. Linnaeus' garden. The lake sparkled in the afternoon sun. The Lords of the Royal Society had decamped to a different part of the garden, Lord Whatley having spotted earlier a rare lizard.

"Though, if you are looking for a motive in Miss Emmeline's death," Mr. Linnaeus said, "I might be able to offer you an idea."

I responded with a raised eyebrow.

"The police came to speak to me about my boat," he began.

"About your boat!?" I exclaimed.

He nodded. "As you know, I had lent my boat to those young men at Monte Verita. The boat is ideal for waterskiing, and since I could never dream of partaking in that particular sport, I enjoyed seeing them use the boat to its best advantage."

I still could not see why the police were interested in the boat, though the drowning came to mind. But how was his boat related to Emmeline's death?

"Now we come to the reason why the police wanted to speak to me," he said, and took another sip of tea. "They were interested in smuggling."

"Smuggling? What do you mean?" The idea was quite unexpected and foreign to me. What would anyone smuggle? From where to where? Of course, I was familiar with prohibition in America and the concept of bootlegging. But there was no prohibition here. I shared my confusion with Mr. Linnaeus.

"No, there is no prohibition," he said, "but it is well known that the locals supplement their meager incomes by smuggling cigarettes and coffee to Italy. Prices for coffee, cigarettes and food staples are quite high in Italy compared to Switzerland. So Swiss people along the border can make a bit of profit smuggling items to Italy. It's not much, but as you've seen, the locals are quite poor. Every little bit helps."

I nodded. I'd noticed the mean stone houses and the modestly dressed locals. That this region of Switzerland was more impoverished than the rest of the country was evident. I wondered about the reasons, but now was not the time to discuss that. "Do you think Spencer, Emmeline and

Nicholas were using your boat for smuggling?" I asked, incredulous.

"I don't think so. It's only the locals who supplement their income this way. Plus, the smuggling around here is quite innocuous. Nothing like what one reads about is happening in America. But it's an interesting theory that the police appear to be exploring. I thought you would want to know, given how fascinated you seem by the girl's death," he said.

I wanted to ask him if he knew anything about the mysterious Brother Gregor, who appeared to have vanished, but I couldn't think of a way of phrasing the question without implying that I suspected Mr. Linnaeus of something nefarious. Plus, the rest of the Royal Society members now returned to the tea table, having been foiled in their attempt to catch a glimpse of the exotic lizard.

After leaving the villa for the day, I spent the evening in my hotel room, going over what I had learned from Mr. Linnaeus and attempting to understand how it related to the information I already had.

I vaguely wondered whether Mr. Linnaeus had been entirely truthful with me, and whether he was somehow involved in smuggling. He had a fast boat, after all, that could outrun any police boat.

The revelation came to me, as all revelations do, in a moment of despair. I'd been struggling to understand why the police would think Emmeline's death had anything to do with smuggling.

And then it struck me. I'd been so silly! Of course! Emmeline and Spencer had been penniless. That I knew for a fact. And perhaps Nicholas was as well. What if they were not smuggling tobacco and polenta but something much more profitable?

Although I had never been tempted to try any, I was well aware that some of our set used narcotics. The newspapers delighted in demonizing all Young Bright Things as cocaine addicts. What if Emmeline and Spencer had used their connections among the upper classes to supply them with cocaine? And with so many of the British upper class vacationing in Italy, it probably was a very lucrative source of income.

The only thing I was not certain about was whether Mr. Linnaeus was involved.

But that night, a note arrived from Wilford, which put all theories of smuggling and narcotics out of my mind. Two things had occurred while I had lounged around the Grand Hotel, cut off from servants' gossip. First, Nicholas had been released from jail due to lack of evidence. Someone from the party had seen him smoking on the verandah during the ball when Emmeline was presumably getting murdered. And second, the Royal Society would not be returning to Monte Verita the following morning because Lord Packenham had been attacked at the commune while trying to sneak a clandestine visit to the bird.

I went to bed with the hazy idea that Nicholas' release and Lord Packenham's attack were somehow connected.

CHAPTER 21

While the next morning I had planned to learn more about the reason behind the attack on Lord Packenham at Monte Verita and how Nicholas might be involved, a young man in uniform deflected my day from its course.

My ongoing correspondence with my chums in London had lulled me into a false sense of serenity, and I had let down my guard against telegrams from London. No longer did I cower when a messenger boy advanced in my direction with a white envelope in hand.

It was thus that I found myself cornered on my way to breakfast by a young hotel chap in red livery and became the unwitting recipient of a telegram from my mother.

Unaware of the disheartening blow he had just delivered on his silver platter, the young messenger held out his hand expectantly. I dropped a few coins in his waiting palm. After all, I could not penalize him for my mother's shortcomings.

I weighed the telegram in my hand. Its heft was suspiciously lacking. Although my mother considered her words worth their weight in gold, she was nevertheless quite generous with them. Why had she spared them for this telegram?

A sense of dread crept up my spine. My mind had just latched on the memory of the last time her telegram was this feeble. A short telegram from my mother was usually the herald of worse things to come—namely, my mother in the flesh. The only time when my mother did not feel compelled to write profusely was when she expected to deliver this profusion in person.

I opened the telegram with bated breath. I scanned it rapidly, looking to get to the fatal blow as swiftly as possible. The quicker I knew when to expect my mother, the quicker I could plan an evasive maneuver.

I looked around furtively. My mother could be stealthy and had been known to send telegrams after she had arrived, thus confusing her victims and allowing them no time to escape.

I listened to the voices coming from the lobby. Could I discern my mother's voice among them? I could not be certain. For an added measure of protection, I pressed my back against a wall. That way, I could not be ambushed by my mother from behind.

Thus somewhat safeguarded, I returned my attention to the telegram. On second reading, it appeared quite benign. I put the telegram down and checked my surroundings again. It could be a trick.

But after a few moments, I decided I was quite safe for now, and proceeded to absorb the contents of the telegram.

It transpired that my mother, having learned of my current whereabouts, had written to a Countess Yablonovna who lived on a small island, San Pancrazio, on Lake Maggiore. The Countess was an acquaintance of my mother's, having met at some charity or other in London. My mother, concerned that I was being starved of intelligent conversation in my uncle's company, had arranged a visit for me to the Countess Yablonovna for tea.

As a boat conveyed me ever-closer to the Countess' island, however, a thought nagged me. There was something quite unnatural in the brevity of my mother's telegram. Had something occurred on the home-front that was preoccupying her? It was quite unlike my mother not to take the opportunity to introduce the subject of my marriage, or lack thereof, into any correspondence. Perhaps there was an eligible bachelor waiting for me on the island. I shuddered. But I had to concede to the cleverness of such a plan—once on the island, I would have no way to escape.

Lost in my thoughts, I was thus quite surprised when the boat turned towards the island I had first noticed from the pier in Ascona, on that dreadful day of the drowning.

From afar, the island had looked overgrown and abandoned. But now I saw that what I had taken for a ruin in the middle of the island was actually a house. With its rough gray stones, thick walls and gothic windows, there was something reminiscent of an abbey about the building. Though crumbling around the edges, it was clear someone lived here.

The second surprise was that groups of young men milled about the overgrown island. And the island itself, on closer inspection, revealed itself to be akin to a tropical paradise with its riots of exotic flowers in bloom. Were the young men gardeners? Why would the Countess be in need of so many?

As the boat neared the dock, it appeared that I was expected. A silent man with rolled-up shirtsleeves led me from the dock, through the gardens, to the gothic pile in the middle of the island and into a grand hallway. The building was cool inside, its thick stone walls keeping out the heat of the day.

The decorations reminded me of a fortress. The furniture was medieval, dark wood and heavy. And everywhere on the walls hung tapestries.

Once I entered the Countess' drawing room, I immediately surmised the reason for my mother's insistence that I meet her. Hanging on the room's wall was the most exquisite medieval tapestry.

Early in her marriage, newly arrived from America, my mother had made the terrible mistake of overpaying for a tapestry she'd thought was rare and exceptional. She had intended to present it as an anniversary gift to my father and had unveiled it during a party in front of all their friends. To her horror and mortification, the tapestry, which the French middleman had assured her was a Gobelin from the middle of the 17th century, turned out to be a 19th century reproduction. My mother was so humiliated by the *faux pas*—because she had unwittingly exposed her New-World ignorance with regards to European history—that gaining knowledge of European art history, and tapestry in particular, became an obsession.

The episode also galvanized her distrust of Frenchmen into a dislike. And it was also the reason why I had been sent to Frau Baumgartnerhoff's finishing school, one of the few such establishments in German-speaking Switzerland, rather than the customary ones in Geneva, in the country's French-speaking territory.

So there I was, staring at a magnificent example of a 15th century tapestry depicting *The Lady and the Unicorn*. I marveled at my mother's network of informants and her ability to track down works of art even on the remotest of islands. I did not dwell on the tapestry for long. After all, I did not want to drive up the price for my mother unnecessarily by showing any interest in the piece. She was quite capable of doing that herself. My mission, as I understood it, though it was never stated explicitly, was to affirm that the piece was indeed as remarkable as had been suggested to my mother. It was.

I now turned my attention to my hostess. A delicate woman of an indeterminate old age, dressed in a heavily embroidered bliaut tunic, she could have easily stepped out of one of her tapestries. She wore her fine graying hair in two long plaits. Her paper-thin skin was stretched over the beautiful bone structure of her face. She must have been superb when young. Her lively eyes belied her age. They were shrewd and observant. Perhaps my mother would find it difficult to get a fair price for the tapestry.

The woman, in her crumbling yet magnificent surroundings, struck me as the personification of genteel poverty.

A maid, as ancient as her mistress, brought in a try with tea things. The Countess poured tea out of a samovar on the sideboard and offered me a cup.

"It was nice of your mother to suggest this visit," the Countess said. She spoke English with a middle-European accent, though I knew her to be Russian.

We exchanged a few pleasantries about my mother and I expressed an interest in learning more about their acquaintance.

"We used to meet at parties. I was not such a recluse when I was younger. Before my English husband abandoned me on this island to go to Italy with his mistress, I traveled often to England."

"I'm sorry," I mumbled.

"Don't be," the Countess chastised me. "I get by well enough. I have my army of young men." She threw a glance towards the mullioned windows and the view beyond.

I felt uneasy asking her about the role of the men on the island and instead decided to ask her about the building.

"It used to be a convent," she said. "In the 13th century, nuns of the Humiliati order built a monastery on the island. The order was suppressed by the 16th century and then the island was abandoned. My husband and I purchased the island about forty years ago. We restored the abbey building and then started planting a botanical garden. We brought in boatloads of soil. The climate here is perfect for tropical and subtropical plants."

She cast her gaze towards the windows again. "I love being surrounded by handsome men. Their virility thrills me," she said quite sincerely.

I looked down at my teacup. I may have blushed.

The Countess' crystal laugh rang across the stone-walled room. "Does my honesty make you uncomfortable? I'm too old to do anything about it," she said and cast a glance towards the windows. "But the men help around in the gardens..."

I wondered how she could afford so many gardeners, but did not vocalize it. "Your gardens are beautiful," I said instead.

"Would you like to take a walk through them?" the Countess said and leaped to her feet with unexpected liveliness.

Although I had no doubt the gardens were attractive and worthy of a visit, it was my curiosity about the gardeners that motivated me to agree most enthusiastically to a stroll through the island.

CHAPTER 22

We walked across fragrant terraces fringed with heavy blooms, along winding paths strewn with petals, through misty groves and down to the lake. Despite the men, the island had an air of peace and tranquility. The jungle-like lushness, together with the crumpling abbey, gave one the impression of opulent decay. It was as though this was a place time forgot.

"Do these men live on the island?" I asked, unable to restrain my curiosity.

"No," the Countess said and walked a little further down the narrow pebbled shore which encircled the island. "They stop off and sometimes overnight on the island. But this is not their home. They help with the gardens when they can."

I didn't follow her meaning. "Why do they stop off here?" I asked. "Where are they going?"

The Countess gave me an inquisitive glance before answering. "Haven't you heard about the smuggling in these parts?" she asked.

Of course! How did I not see it before? These men weren't gardeners, they were smugglers!

I responded with an equivocal smile.

"The island makes a good base for the men's incursions into Italy. I receive a small cut of their profits," the Countess said without reserve.

We walked along the beach in silence.

"The men also bring me news," she said after a few moments. "I'm cut off from the world...by choice. But one shouldn't become too insular, even if one lives on an island...The young people from Monte Verita used to come and see me, but less and less these days...so many of them come and go...so now I get my news from the smugglers..."

The mention of Monte Verita made me think of Emmeline's murder, and I wondered if the Countess had heard about it.

She nodded. "And I heard about the man who drowned," she added. "So much tragedy in our peaceful slice of paradise. The lake demands its offering sometimes..." She let her gaze glide over the surface of the water. "Both were English, I believe?" she asked and turned to me.

I nodded in return.

I wanted to tell her that Spencer and Emmeline had been husband and wife, but somehow, it didn't seem right to make their secret public.

"We had an English man spend a few nights on the island recently," she added.

The revelation startled me.

The Countess must have observed my reaction because she said, "I rarely take notice of the men who overnight here. But my head gardener told me that there was an Englishman on the island. He was diverted by the novelty of it and felt inclined to share the news with me."

My mind jumped to the missing Brother Gregor. "Do you know who he was?" I asked.

"As the smugglers seemed to know him and accepted him as part of their camp, I didn't see a reason to enquire about him any further."

I tried to hide my disappointment. "Can you think of the exact dates?" I asked instead. If Brother Gregor had been hiding out on the island, it would explain why we hadn't heard anything more about him.

The Countess thought for a moment. "Funny you should ask," she said. "I remember thinking how rather odd was the coincidence of an Englishman stopping off on the island at the same time as an English woman dying. It made me wonder if all was well at Monte Verita..." She gazed for a while at the undulating water. Then she turned to me. "That would mean that he was here at about the time the young woman was killed," she said, as though just realizing it.

"Did you not tell anyone?" I asked, trying not to betray my surprise.

"The authorities, you mean?" she asked, a momentary smile playing on her lips. I nodded. "We try to stay out of each other's way," the Countess said with an impish sparkle in her eyes. "I do not want them poking around the island, for obvious reasons."

"So you didn't meet the Englishman while he was on the island? You didn't attempt to find out what he was doing here?" I asked incredulously. I couldn't help but think that the Countess had hosted the killer on her island.

"No. I didn't want to pry," she said in a calm voice that was so unlike the tumult of questions and feelings that had broken out inside me. "Everyone has something that they want to keep private," she concluded with a shrug.

"But weren't you afraid?" I asked, disbelief coloring in my voice.

"Of what?" she countered undisturbed.

"There is a murderer about," I said. I could feel my eyebrows riding ever higher on my forehead in astonishment at the Countess' indifference.

The Countess dismissed my anxiety with a flick of her delicate hand. "But what is that to do with me?" she said.

I knew it was a rhetorical question.

"One of the reasons young men like stopping off on the island," she continued, "is because I don't ask who they are and where they are from. I only ask that they contribute to the garden work. My head gardener, Angelo, is getting on in age, so he appreciates the help. I leave it up to him to deal with the men."

We made our way along the stony beach in silence. It was clear that the Countess was reluctant to say anything further about the Englishman, even if she knew more. But despite the Countess' unconcerned manner, I could not so easily dismiss the first real clue I'd stumbled upon concerning Brother Gregor's whereabouts.

A dark mass ahead on the beach stood out among the white pebbles—the remnants of a fire.

"Left by the smugglers who camp out here overnight," the Countess said, noticing my interest in the scorched stone circle.

A vague thought crossed my mind, and I picked up a stick. I prodded through the charred remains of the extinguished fire—branches, logs, and broken boat planks. The Countess was watching me closely, but did not interrupt. A glint of silver among the ashes caught my eye, and for a moment my heart leaped with joy. But alas, it proved to be a discarded can.

Disappointed, I tossed the stick to the side and walked on. It had been a long shot. I'd hoped that Emmeline's killer, if he'd indeed been camping out on the island, might have attempted to burn the camera and its evidence…If indeed he had stolen it…Perhaps my search for the camera was futile…

I turned to my hostess. "Do you think your gardener might know more about the Englishman?" I asked. I was desperate to learn more about the man who had camped out on the island at the time of Emmeline's murder.

The Countess regarded me for a moment with

faint amusement, but did not pry.

We walked back into the coolness of the house. The gardener was called, and he arrived at one of the French windows of the drawing room. He was twisting a cap in his hands and concern had twisted the weather-beaten features on his face. His skin was dark and leathery, the result of a life spent outside among the elements. He apologized for bringing dirt into the Countess' room, or so I assumed by his gestures pointing to his muddy trousers and boots.

The Countess waved off his worries and asked him some questions. I strained to understand, trying to discern any Latin words, but his dialect was as twisted as his cap. I did not recognize the language as Italian.

"He says that he knows the gentleman we are speaking of," the Countess turned to me. "He was definitely an Englishman. He could tell by the accent."

"Does he know his name?" I asked.

The gardener shook his head. And then added something.

"He doesn't know his name, and neither do the other men. Smugglers are reticent by necessity. But he's sure he was from Monte Verita."

"What did the man look like?" I asked, full of

hope. Even if he didn't know the man's name, surely he could describe him.

"Like an Englishman," the Countess translated after much gesturing on the gardener's part. "All Englishmen look the same to him," she added.

The gardener looked down at his muddy boots as though sensing that he was not as helpful as I had hoped.

I nodded, trying to hide my dejection.

"Can he remember if the man was here on the night the woman was killed at the villa?" I said.

He shook his head when the Countess put the question to him. He stepped nervously and twisted his cap a bit more while replying to her. I had a feeling I would owe the man a new cap by the time we were through with the questions.

The Countess turned to me. "He can't be sure. So many men come and go. He doesn't keep track of them."

I sighed. Was the old gardener hiding something? "Countess, you said the other smugglers knew him. Where had they met him before?" I asked.

She posed the question to the gardener. He gave what looked to me like an equivocal answer. His head moved from side to side, and his hand wobbled to emphasize the uncertainty of his answer. I didn't hold out much hope of getting a definitive answer.

"Some men from Monte Verita have been using

the smuggling trails. They've met him on the trail. But they know little more about him," the Countess said.

The unexpected revelation startled me. Here was conclusive proof that the Monte Verita people were involved in smuggling. The police were correct in their suspicions, I mused. Perhaps Brother Gregor's hermit episodes were a cover for the smuggling. Had Spencer and Nicholas also been on the trail with Brother Gregor?

"But the smugglers cannot tell me the identity of the man on the island or of the Englishmen using the smuggling trail?" I asked.

The gardener shook his head and avoided my gaze. I could sense that the old man was nervous about something. Perhaps he didn't want strangers like me to know too much about what was happening on the island.

The Countess dismissed the gardener, but as he left, he looked back nervously at me. I wondered what worried him.

"So, you see," the Countess said, cutting into my thoughts with a bright voice, "there is nothing to worry about. It's just someone from Monte Verita stopping off."

My countenance must have betrayed my disappointment because the Countess added, "Don't mistake Angelo's inability to help you for unwillingness to do so. He's almost blind in one eye and more concerned with greenfly than anything else," she said kindly. "Plus, even if some of the men had recognized your Englishman, they would not part with the information so easily. The smugglers keep a low profile and, in turn, do not pry into other people's affairs."

I concluded that Brother Gregor had picked an ideal location to hide out. It was the only place in the region where no one would pay the slightest attention to him.

One thing that the old gardener had said, however, had caught my attention. It was the fact that since the smugglers had recognized the Englishman, he must have been a regular on the smuggling trail. What were these English people at Monte Verita up to?

"Countess, do you suppose the people from Monte Verita are smuggling something across the border?" I asked.

She shook her head. "I do not know, my dear."

I was crestfallen. I doubted whether the Countess would confide in me even if she knew. Perhaps the Countess' discretion was the island's chief attraction for the smugglers. Or perhaps she was implicated...

The Countess gave me a start as she sprang to her feet and clapped her hands. "I have a marvelous idea," she said. "If you join me tomorrow on a little boat excursion, I might be able to help you shed some light on what these Englishmen could be doing on the smugglers' trail."

That evening, I left the island with a head full of ideas and suppositions, and giddy with anticipation. But I was also aware of a different sentiment swirling inside me—I could not subdue the feeling that I had perceived something of importance on the island. What that was, however, I could not recollect.

CHAPTER 23

Early the next morning, the Countess, and a dashing young Italian man who was driving the small motorboat, picked me up at a dock near Locarno's steamboat terminal. As we set off in the direction of the Countess' island, I wondered where she was taking me.

But at the back of my mind, a small thought was still troubling me. Who had attacked Lord Packenham and to what end? But as I believed that today's excursion held the answers to all my questions, I pushed the thought aside. And since Lord Packenham was not my favorite member of the Royal Society, I reasoned that the investigation into his attack was a matter for the police. I vaguely wondered if the other members of the Royal Society were in danger of being attacked, but as the Royal Society had paused its visits to Monte Verita for the moment, and as Lord Packenham was by far the least likable of the members, I concluded my uncle was safe.

It was thus with a clear conscience that I turned to the Countess and asked her where we were going. I had not failed to notice that we had bypassed her island and were now driving down the lake towards what I assumed was Italy.

"We're off to the Italian border," she said.

As the driver turned the boat towards the steep cliffs visible on one side of the lake, the Countess pointed towards a yellow house, no different from a small Italianate villa, perched on the rocks.

"Despite its imposing architecture," she said, "the building lacks running water and electricity, and is inaccessible by any road. Only by water."

"What is it?" I asked, intrigued.

"The building houses the Swiss border control and is home to the border guard," she explained. "He patrols the lake. Others guard the hills and mountains."

Mindful of the Countess' association with the local smugglers, I voiced my surprise that we were about to visit the border guard.

"Oh, let not the fact that I harbor smugglers on my little island fool you," she said with a smile, "Signor Caviano and I are old friends."

The Countess explained that the local Swiss border guards usually turned a blind eye to the smuggling activities of their compatriots. After all, the smugglers were their neighbors. Since the flow of goods was from Switzerland to Italy, the smuggling did not have a negative effect on the locals. In fact, it was good for the local merchants and shop-keepers. Though Swiss authorities from the north complained about it, the local border guards saw no reason to discourage it.

A uniformed man with a peaked cap lowered over his eyes to keep out the sun's glare met us at the dock. His dark hair and thick, dark mustache reminded me of the senior policeman I had met at Mr. Linnaeus' villa. But as greetings, introductions and local gossip were exchanged, Signor Caviano proved to be an affable man. His paunch and ruddy cheeks also spoke to his generous nature, towards the enjoyment of food and drink.

Signor Caviano invited us to sit under the vine-covered pergola in his small garden. He served us thick coffee in diminutive cups which he had prepared in a pot over open fire. If he was surprised by the reason for our visit, he didn't show it. Indeed, he seemed to enjoy having company and a captive audience for his border patrol anecdotes.

After a few jolly stories about upturned tourist trunks and floating ladies' undergarments in the lake, the Countess, who served as my translator, stirred the conversation towards smuggling.

To my question about whether people from Monte Verita were involved in smuggling, the border guard inclined his head noncommittally. I took the gesture as a confirmation that he knew something about it.

"I'm looking for a young man who stayed on the Countess' island a few days ago. I think he might know something about the death of the English woman at the villa in Locarno," I said.

Signor Caviano nodded and crossed himself.

"Yes, I heard about the poor woman," he said through my translator. "And now that poor man." He crossed himself again.

"What poor man?" the Countess and I asked in unison.

"Haven't you heard?" the border guard asked, surprised. But the emotion was quickly eclipsed by the obvious delight he took in being the bearer of unexpected news. The pleasure doubled by the fact that the news was grim. He refilled our cups with the undrinkable sludge and only imparted the particulars about the "poor man" after he'd sat back down and taken a long sip of sediment. An involuntary shudder passed through my body as I watched him swallow his coffee with pleasure. "An Englishman has disappeared, presumed dead, on the smuggling trail," he finally said. "Locals found his rucksack," he said. "But no body has been found." He shrugged. "It happens in the mountains," he concluded.

My mind jumped to the missing Brother Gregor. Had he fallen to his death? Is that why he had disappeared so suddenly?

"But why do you presume he's dead?" I asked.

"Because his rucksack and a few personal items were found on the side of a trail notorious for accidents. No one who falls down that cliff comes back up alive," he said.

"So, no one has gone to look for his body?" I asked. How can the locals be sure he's dead if there was no body?

He shook his head. "The local lads will not risk their own lives to recover the body. It's too unsafe."

So many questions were swirling through my mind. "When did it happen?" I said.

"It must have happened at some point yesterday evening or during the night. They only discovered the rucksack this morning," said Signor Caviano. "Perhaps he took a break and slipped. It happens." He shrugged. "Mind you, the lads have been talking about an Englishman camping on the trail for the past few days..." he trailed off and gazed at the water as though lost in thought.

"How did you hear about it?" I asked. With no electricity and no roads, how did the border guard learn about the disappearance?

"One of the fishermen told me this morning," he said. "His son was in the party that discovered the rucksack."

"But how do they know it was an Englishman and not one of the locals?" I asked.

Signor Caviano shook his head. "Only Englishmen carry these rucksacks," he said with certitude. "Plus, there were some personal items in the rucksack as well."

Though I was certain that the Englishman was Brother Gregor, I asked Signor Caviano about the man's identity.

Signor Caviano gestured noncommittally with his hands. "Give me a minute. It was a nice Italian name, which surprised me. Not Guido, not Enzo... Nico!."

I gasped. "Nicholas...but that's impossible... why is Brother Gregor..." The revelation was startling. Why was Nicholas on the smugglers' trail? Had he really slipped or had someone pushed him? Brother Gregor? What if the locals were unhappy about the Englishmen using their smuggling trail? That was a possibility I had not explored.

"Were the locals upset that the Englishmen from Monte Verita were encroaching on their trail?" I asked, thinking back to the angry locals the police, and even Poppy, had mentioned. "Do you think one of the locals could have pushed Nicholas?" I asked. *And strangled Emmeline*, I wanted to add, but didn't.

The border guard shook his head vigorously. "No, no!" he exclaimed. "It could not be."

"Why?" I asked. After all, it was not unreasonable to think that if one were running a smuggling operation, one would get angry if foreigners moved into one's smuggling territory and became one's competition. I knew I would be displeased with such a turn of events. "What makes you so sure that it could not be one of the locals?" I pressed.

Signor Caviano shrugged. "They don't mind having the Englishmen there," he said.

"They don't?" I asked, surprised. Was this

something to do with honor among thieves or the like? Although these people weren't really thieves...

"No." He shook his head again. "You see, they were not involved in smuggling the same things as the locals," he said and lowered his voice.

I raised an eyebrow at the revelation. *I'd guessed correctly!* This was about narcotics. "Were they involved in smuggling cocaine?" I asked, leaning forward and lowering my voice to match his.

"No!" the border guard replied, outraged once the Countess had translated my question. His outcry startled me. And then I wondered if he was perhaps protesting a bit too energetically. But even the Countess looked at me as though astonished by my suggestion. "God-fearing people live in this region!" Signor Caviano said passionately and crossed himself. "No one on my watch is involved in such devilish work!"

"Forgive me," I said, my face burning with mortification. "I didn't mean to imply that the local men are involved in smuggling narcotics. Only that the Englishmen might be. You said they weren't smuggling food or tobacco. I just assumed..."

"Young lady," the border guard said and straightened up, "I turn a blind eye to the men of the region bringing food stuff across the border because they are not hurting anyone. They are helping their Italian brethren to get food at cheaper prices. But I would not stand for anything like cocaine or opiates to cross the border with my knowledge." The jollity had gone from his eyes. I could see that I had hurt his feelings and his pride.

I nodded and apologized again. I needed to tread carefully, but my thoughts were running wild. If it was not cocaine, what could it be? Jewels, guns, liquor as in America? "Do you know what the Englishmen were bringing across the border?" I asked cautiously.

He gazed at me sternly, and I wondered if he would tell me. "Books," he said.

"Books?" asked the Countess, astounded. She had been following the development with as much interest as I had.

The border guard nodded. Some of the previous liveliness returned to his eyes. He seemed to revel in the surprise his unexpected revelation had elicited. My transgression was forgotten.

"But why would anyone smuggle books?" I asked, still unsure if I, or rather the Countess, had understood him correctly.

"Can you not think of a reason?" asked the Countess. She sat back, self-satisfied. She had gleaned something that was still eluding me.

While I loved riddles and puzzles and was known to be an accomplished scavenger hunt champion, I had to admit that I could see no reason why anyone would smuggle books across the border to Italy. What was the Countess alluding to that I could not see?

"Monte Verita is home to some prominent radical thinkers," the Countess said. "Among them are many who sympathize with communist ideas and the plight of workers in Italy. I would think that more than a few of Monte Verita's residents would be opposed to Mussolini's regime and would look for ways to support Mussolini's opponents in Italy."

I began to comprehend. I had witnessed firsthand, only a few weeks ago, during my stay in Italy, the unpleasantness of the Mussolini regime. "So, you mean the Englishmen were buying books here in Switzerland and smuggling them to Italy?"

"Yes," the border guard confirmed. "But not buying books. Printing them. Books and newspapers full of ideas that Mussolini would not approve of."

"I would think the Italian border guards would be keen to stop such ideas from crossing into Italy," added the Countess. Signor Caviano nodded.

This new piece of information was unexpected. But I would examine it more closely once back at the hotel.

We spoke for a few more minutes. Neither Signor Caviano nor the Countess could think why Emmeline or Nicholas might have been murdered for their books. Or by whom.

I thanked the border guard for his time and made a small contribution to his refreshments fund.

As the boat drove away from the border house, I wondered if Emmeline and Nicholas had been killed because they were trying to bring radical ideas into Italy. Had some Mussolini sympathizers killed them?

"It's possible," said the Countess when I put the question to her. "There is a strong underground movement among Italian-speaking Swiss who want to split away from Switzerland and join Italy. There are quite a few fascist outfits in the region, printing newspapers and books, spreading Mussolini's ideas. The Swiss authorities are just as keen to prevent fascist ideas from spreading in Switzerland as the Italians are to stop communist ideas from establishing themselves in Italy."

As we got closer to Locarno, I wondered if the deaths of Emmeline and Nicholas were due to some sort of ideological turf war between Communists and Fascists. And if so, where did the missing Englishman, Brother Gregor, fit in? Was he the hand behind all of these killings?

CHAPTER 24

Following my visit to the border guard, I spent the time after lunch walking along Locarno's lakeside promenade, trying to put all the pieces of the puzzle together.

What I had thought was a lovers' triangle had turned out to be a smuggling ring. But not the smuggling of anything illicit, the smuggling of revolutionary ideas in the form of books. Were Emmeline and Nicholas murdered because of these books? And was Nicholas' disappearance really murder? Perhaps he'd wished to vanish for a while and staged his fall. After all, there was only his rucksack as evidence that he had fallen over the side of the cliff.

I had to concede that while my trips to the Countess' island and the border guard's house had supplied me with some tantalizing information, they had also left me with many unanswered questions. I still didn't know what role Brother Gregor, if any, played in this ordeal.

And how did Lord Packenham fit in the puzzle? Why had he been attacked at Monte Verita? His countenance when he had seen Emmeline floated back to me. Why had he been so surprised to see her? Was he perhaps a supporter and a financier of Mussolini's regime? Lord Packenham was certainly unlikable enough to believe him capable of it. But a murderer? I shook my head. That was surely not possible.

Perhaps I needed to find out more about the books that were being smuggled into Italy. I needed to find out where they were being printed. But with Spencer, Emmeline, Nicholas and Brother Gregor gone, I wondered who at Monte Verita would know.

I posed the conundrum to Poppy, who, having joined me for afternoon tea at the Grand Hotel, was now on her way back to the commune. I was accompanying her on the blue tram as far as its terminus. She agreed to do a bit of sleuthing on my behalf.

As the tram left Piazza Grande and was about to enter the narrow confines of Via Rinaldo Simen, I spotted Lord Packenham. He was walking down the street in the company of a dapper young man. The young man reminded me vaguely of someone, but I'd failed to see him properly as the tram had gone by.

"Oh!" Poppy exclaimed and leaned across me to look out of the tram's window at the men's retreating backs. "There's Brother Gregor!"

As the tram continued to crawl down the street, I looked back at the young man walking beside

Lord Packenham. *Surely that could not be Brother Gregor!* I thought.

"But how can that be?" I asked Poppy, confused. "Brother Gregor has long hair and a long beard." The man walking beside Lord Packenham was well-groomed and wore a well-cut suit.

"I'm positive, Gassy!" Poppy insisted. "That's Brother Gregor, only without his beard. He must have shaved it off since leaving Monte Verita."

I stared back at the man as the tram pulled us slowly away from him. Poppy had many faults, but her ability to recognize handsome young men of her acquaintance—even when they were in disguise—was flawless.

Emboldened by Poppy's revelation, I grabbed Poppy's hand, shouted at the tram conductor to request a stop and jumped off the moving carriage before it had come to a halt. The conductor wished us a good day, or something along those lines in Italian, but I had no time for pleasantries.

Poppy followed without too many objections. We crossed the street and hid in the shadows of the grand entryway of a palazzo.

"What's going on, Gassy?" Poppy asked. I could sense by a steely note in her voice that she was struggling to maintain her unquestioning faith in my actions.

"I want to see what Lord Packenham is up to," I said. *If Poppy was correct, and this was Brother Gregor, what was Lord Packenham doing in his company?*

"Why should Lord Packenham be up to anything?" she asked.

"He's been acting strangely lately," I said. Poppy raised an eyebrow. "More strangely than usual," I amended.

"Yes. Now that you mention it, before he was attacked at Monte Verita, he'd been coming quite often," Poppy said.

"To do what?" I asked, confounded by the revelation.

"Now, Gassy," Poppy said in a tone that tutors reserve for particularly obtuse pupils in their care, "the community is sworn to secrecy. Guests come to Monte Verita for complete rejuvenation in absolute privacy." She stuck her nose up in the air, letting me know that objections were futile.

It was a gesture I was well familiar with. But this was not boarding school. "Poppy," I said, exasperated, "you are not a stakeholder in that enterprise. You are not bound by any secrecy." I rolled my eyes to underline my point.

"Perhaps you are right. In any case, the community seems to be a bit unhappy with my continued involvement. I've heard a few grumblings about the rigor of my regime and unyielding program of communal duties…"

I failed to hear the rest of her narrative as I was concentrating on moving unobserved down the street, from doorway to doorway, hiding in the shadows of the entranceways.

"Oh, blast it!" I exclaimed. Lord Packenham and the young man had entered into a local drinking establishment. From a recent experience, I had learned that unlike in England, here ladies did not seem to be welcome in public houses. The one time I had made the mistake of entering a tavern to order a lemonade, I was stared down by the exclusively male patrons and speedily ushered out by the proprietor.

The obliging concierge at the Grand Hotel—after regaining his composure, aided by a tall glass of soda water and loosening of the tie—had lowered his startled eyebrows sufficiently to explain that in Italian-speaking Switzerland men and women did not consume beverages in the same establishments. It transpired that local ladies only ventured to drink lemonade in cafes and pastry shops. And some allowed themselves this luxury only on Sundays.

Thus, I knew we could not follow Lord Packenham into the tavern.

But all was not lost. Though we could not follow them in, I had managed to see the young man's face clearly as he had gone into the drinking establishment, and recognized him.

"So, why are we following them?" Poppy asked, and she attempted to squeeze her bulk into a particularly narrow doorway.

"Because the person you claim is Brother

Gregor is, in fact, Lord Packenham's son, Ludovic!"
I exclaimed.

CHAPTER 25

With Poppy safely stowed on a donkey cart to Monte Verita, I hurried back to Mr. Linnaeus' villa. I marveled at the fact that I hadn't recognized Ludovic the first time I had seen him at Monte Verita. The beard and long hair had completely transformed him. Plus, now that I thought about it, I had not seen him socially since before the war. I wondered how long he had lived at Monte Verita.

Brother Gregor's true identity explained Lord Packenham's reaction at Monte Verita on our first visit, but it still left many questions unanswered. I was on my way to find James and see if he could shed some light on the mystery.

Why had Ludovic left Monte Verita so abruptly after seeing his father? Why had Lord Packenham continued going to Monte Verita outside of the Royal Society visits, even when his son had not been there? Who had attacked Lord Packenham and for what reason? Why had Ludovic denounced his Monte Verita persona? And most importantly, was Ludovic the murderer?

I was no longer certain that Ludovic had been part of the Spencer-Emmeline-Nicholas lovers' triangle. I was now convinced that I had misinterpreted his gaze during my first visit to Monte Verita. He had been looking at Lord Packenham, not Emmeline. But I was still unclear about his involvement in the smuggling of subversive books. *Could the son of Lord Packenham be involved in some sort of radical movement?* I wondered. Lord Packenham's conservative temperament certainly seemed to invite rebellious behavior in his children.

As I rode the funicular up to the villa, another memory floated up in my mind. I remembered James eavesdropping at Monte Verita on my conversation with Poppy regarding Brother Gregor. It seemed likely James had known all this time that Brother Gregor was Ludovic. Why had he kept it secret from me?

My thoughts drifted to James. I had seen much less of him on this trip than I would have liked and had interpreted his conduct as a signal that he no longer wished to maintain our friendship. But perhaps he had been preoccupied with this Lord Packenham-Ludovic business. Whatever that might be.

Why was Lord Packenham being so secretive about his son? Was it simply that his son had been a resident at Monte Verita, or was there something more?

Where had Ludovic been since leaving Monte Verita? Had he been hiding out on the Countess' island? Had he pushed Nicholas down the cliff?

But another problem remained. If it was Ludovic that Emmeline had seen at the ball, why had she been so frightened of him? Why had his presence at the ball unnerved her so? She had seen him many times before at Monte Verita. Had she failed to recognize him until the night of the ball? Had the long hair and beard been enough to disguise his true identity at Monte Verita? *The disguise had been enough to fool me,* I conceded.

And what was the connection between Ludovic, Emmeline and Nicholas? What had precipitated the murders of Emmeline and Nicholas? And did Lord Packenham play a role in any of this?

Mr. Linnaeus' butler was quite obliging and was able to locate James without delay.

James listened to my carefully constructed thesis about Ludovic as Brother Gregor, as the man on the Countess' island, as a smuggler of books, and as a murderer. Though even I had to admit that the murder argument was a bit flimsy.

He gazed at me for a while. He then stepped away from me and shook his head. I could see that he was trying to make up his mind to tell me something. Thoughts and emotions, like stormy clouds, battled across his face. Even when troubled, James' face was irresistibly attractive.

Observing him, I could sense that he was wrestling with a moral dilemma. Would he confess to having suspected all along that Lord Packenham's son was behind the murders?

He shook his head once again. "No, Caroline. I know you are quite good at puzzles, but this time you are entirely wrong," he said calmly.

I wanted to scream and shake him, but that would not do. "What do you mean?" I said instead, trying to keep my voice as level as his.

"I simply mean that your theory is wrong. Ludovic is not the murderer," he explained.

"But how can you be sure? What makes you so sure he is not?" I asked, my voice rising.

He had made his way towards me, but now stepped away again and walked to the far end of the room. "I cannot divulge that information," he said. He turned to look at me. "Just trust me when I tell you he cannot be the killer." His eyes bored into me across the room.

I felt myself faltering in my conviction of Ludovic's guilt under his gaze. "And you are not going to tell me what makes you so certain of his innocence?" I asked.

"No," he said simply.

Aargh! "Then I am going to continue to believe that Ludovic is the killer," I said. I felt like a petulant child, but couldn't help myself.

"As you wish," he retorted.

I was not ready to give up so easily. "Just give me a hint," I said, "and I would be prepared to accept your assurance that he is not guilty." I attempted not to grovel. Instead, I smiled at him, and adopted that look in my eyes that usually made young men rush by my side with drinks at house parties.

James merely scowled. He was infuriating. I truly was ready to accept his standpoint on the subject of Ludovic, if he would only give me an indication of the information he possessed that made him so certain Ludovic was innocent.

"Caroline," he said in a gentle voice. I beamed at him. I knew I had worn him down. "Please do not ask me any more questions. I cannot answer them," he said with finality.

My breath caught. That was not the outcome I had expected.

In the next moment, blood rushed to my head. James was so impossible sometimes! Was he even truly my friend? And how silly of me to have hoped that one day we could be more than friends.

Waves of vexation washed over me. I turned on my heel, sent him a deprecating look over my shoulder—so he would be left in no doubt of how I felt about him at the present moment—and stormed out of the room.

But as I was about to slam the door, my mind began to race. Who was James protecting? Why would he not reveal at least some of what he knew? Was he protecting Ludovic? Or was he actually protecting Lord Packenham?

Ha! I screamed internally. I'd always suspected that Lord Packenham was a bad egg. Only those who were guilty of some great moral transgression hid behind a facade of unwavering morality.

I resolved to seek out my uncle's help once again.

CHAPTER 26

Uncle Albert was a fascinating man. He had the capacity to remember that narrowleaf stoneseed, golden puccoon and fringed gromwell were the same plant, *Lithospermum incisum*, but sometimes more practical knowledge escaped him.

But on this occasion, I had full confidence in his ability to retain and relay gossip pertaining to the Royal Society. Furthermore, since Lord Packenham was not one of Uncle Albert's favorite Society members, if my uncle knew of any misdemeanors on Lord Packenham's part, I was certain he would have no qualms about divulging them to me.

My uncle's precarious relationship with the Royal Society's members and the unrelenting rivalry among them was a boon to me on this occasion.

After enquiring about his health and the state of his correspondence, which I'd ignored for some days now, I plunged straight in. "Uncle, do you get the impression that Lord Packenham has been acting somewhat out of character on this trip?"

"Has he?" my uncle asked faintly. Was I imagining it, or was there a note of evasiveness in my uncle's voice? "More than usual?" he asked feebly, as though to clarify.

I nodded.

"No, no." He shook his head. "I have noticed nothing unusual," he said, his voice inflecting into a steely defiance.

I sensed that Uncle Albert was hiding something. Normally, he would have taken any opportunity to denounce his rival. Why was my uncle shielding Lord Packenham? Did Lord Packenham have some hold over my uncle? Was he blackmailing dear Uncle Albert into silence?

But before I could pose a question about any such devious scheme on Lord Packenham's part, I inspected my uncle more closely. The stooped countenance, the shifty eyes darting between the tassels of his slippers, the nervous picking at a loose thread on his embroidered smoking jacket, all gave me to understand that he was not guarding a secret about Lord Packenham. He was safeguarding some sort of embarrassment of his own.

I threw a furtive glance at Wilford, but at this moment he wore the countenance of a Musketeer of the Guard—nothing could persuade him to betray my uncle's confidence.

I sat down at the writing desk at the far end of my uncle's sitting room. The distance afforded me a perfect view of my uncle and—dare I say?—clarity.

I scrutinized him. My uncle's healthy tan and

uncharacteristic lack of psoriasis were suspicious.

And then I knew what my uncle was attempting to conceal.

Poppy, relenting on her vow of secrecy towards visitors to Monte Verita this afternoon, had related the most singular facts to me. On any given morning, soon after the sun rose over the crest of the Alps in the east, and before its rays licked the ripples across the calm waters of Lake Maggiore, a casual observer could witness the most curious sight. Along the twisting road that wound its way up the hill from the village of Ascona to Monte Verita, a procession of sorts could be discerned among the tall palm trees and towering cypresses.

If one were to look more closely, the most unlikely caravan would present itself. There, along the dirt road, as though a caravan across the desert, donkeys made their slow ascent.

Scrutinizing the caravan even closer, the casual observer would notice two curious points. One, that the donkeys traveled at a moderate distance from one another, such that, thanks to the bends in the road, none was visible to the others. And two, that each donkey was carrying a member of the Royal Society for Natural History Appreciation on its back.

The men started off from Locarno under the cover of darkness and arrived in Ascona just as the sun crested over the hump of the Alps. So unvarying was their procession each morning that the locals had started taking their morning break earlier in order to watch the caravan. The locals were also doing a booming business in donkeys for hire.

I admit that the description of this daily cavalcade baffled me until Poppy explained that among the residents of Monte Verita was a disciple of the naturopath Arnold Rikli. I needed a quick refresher on the topic of Arnold Rikli, and Poppy obliged by clarifying that Mr. Rikli had made his name as something of a holistic healer.

The treatment Mr. Rikli was best known for was sunbathing in the nude.

Poppy could not recall which member of the Royal Society had discovered the treatment first, but news of its efficacy on rheumatic joints, skin ailments, asthma and various illnesses caused by nervous dispositions or gluttony spread like eczema among the rest of the members of the Society.

Thus, it transpired that each morning the members of the Royal Society made their way up to Monte Verita to spend a few hours in specially designed sun huts, interspersed among the meadows. And the secretive procession could be chalked up to each member's unwillingness to admit to undergoing such sun therapies.

While the ritual did wonders for the complexions of the Royal Society's members, it also afforded a welcome respite from the daily drudgery for the fishermen and farmers of Ascona.

Having thus surmised the root cause of my uncle's equivocal behavior, I proceeded to test my theory.

"Dear uncle," I said reassuringly, "do not fret that I am in any way interested in the practices of the members of the Royal Society as a whole. I am only partial to what Lord Packenham may have to hide."

My uncle perked up, and the light of reason returned to his eyes. "Ah! Yes! Of course! I know exactly what you are referring to. Never liked the fellow. Where should I begin?"

I had struck gold. "Begin at the beginning, I suppose," I said with a note of satisfaction in my voice. I settled back in my chair as a wave of tranquility washed over my body. My uncle was about to divulge all.

"Well, to start off, Lord Packenham is a graduate of Harrow. Not an Old Etonian, you see?" My uncle underlined the importance of this fact by tapping the side of his nose. "Then, to make matters worse, his title comes from the cadet line of the family. I, for one, would refuse a title if it was bestowed upon me through only a cadet line." My uncle cast me another meaningful glance. He looked like he was just warming up for what promised to be a marathon event.

But the more he spoke about Lord Packenham,

the more I doubted that he had anything of value to contribute to my present investigation.

After listening for a while to Uncle Albert enumeration of Lord Packenham's various shortcomings—from his inability to recognize a hairy woodpecker from a downy one, and possessing only three of the requisite four volumes of Francis Trevelyan Buckland's *Curiosities of Natural History*—I determined that my uncle required some prompting in order to concentrate his thoughts on the problem at hand. Namely, Lord Packenham's political leanings, his son's presence at Monte Verita, and the family's association with Emmeline and Nicholas.

"That's all very fascinating," I told my uncle, "but do you know of any secrets pertaining to Lord Packenham's political views?"

"Politics?" my uncle asked. "That's not something we discuss at the Royal Society, Caroline," he said sternly.

I nodded. I was not about to be defeated. "Do you know anything about Lord Packenham's son, Ludovic?" I asked.

"He has a son?" my uncle asked. The note of astonishment in his voice did not escape me. "I didn't know he had it in him," he said and shook his head.

I faltered for a moment, but pressed on. "Yes. And his son was, until recently, a resident at Monte Verita, going under the name of Brother Gregor."

"Was he, by Jove?" my uncle said. He transferred his gaze to his tassels again. "No, I'm not familiar with his brother..."

The lapse made me realize that the mention of the infernal commune had caused the aged relation to clam up once more. His escapades under the sun at Monte Verita were perhaps a topic the old boy preferred to keep close to his heart.

I sighed in resignation and turned my attention to the three-days' worth of correspondence stacked on the desk.

It wasn't until I was taking my leave that Wilford, who escorted me to the door, said, "If I may be so bold as to make a suggestion. I believe you may find the answer you are looking for if you were to ask Miss Kettering-Thrapston to inquire about an angry patriarch who resides in Ascona, who has been implicated in various attacks on the Monte Verita community. And about a missing servant girl from the aforementioned community."

It was with a spring in my step that I made my way to the funicular that evening. It appeared that even revolutionary radicals living in bohemian communities needed servants to change their bed linens.

189

CHAPTER 27

Thus emboldened by the cryptic message from Wilford, I made my way to Ascona and Monte Verita the next morning.

Preferring to forgo the tram and donkey cart rides necessary to reach the commune, I decided to cover the distance on a bicycle secured from the hotel.

As I pumped the pedals, I lamented, and not for the first time, the utter inconvenience of the lack of a telephone at Monte Verita. For a conversation that could have been conducted over the telephone, from the comfort of the conference room I had commandeered at the hotel, I had to travel instead all the way to Ascona.

I found Poppy bullying a hapless chap into submission over some new scheme she had devised for the vegetable patch. The bearded chap, whose face had become as white as the loose robe he was wearing, regained some of his color when I led Poppy away.

"Now, tell me, Poppy," I began, and threaded my arm through hers to steer her away from descending upon another chap in a toga that was setting up the communal breakfast table, "have you heard any gossip about a missing servant girl at Monte Verita?"

"What? No!" she protested, "I have had none of the local help quit during my tenure here!"

Her unreserved denial led me to believe that a mutiny might be brewing among the locals employed as help at Monte Verita. And I had no doubt that Poppy's brand of supervision was the root cause of it. The sooner the members of the Royal Society concluded their observations of the infernal brown bird, the sooner I could lead Poppy away from impending doom.

Although, come to think of it, now that Nicholas was no longer at the commune, Poppy's original mission was over. But as Monte Verita seemed to hold a few secrets still, perhaps Poppy remaining here could continue to be useful.

"I got the impression that the girl disappeared a while back, before you got here," I said, trying to appease her. "Wilford suggested she might be somehow implicated in the mystery of Ludovic and the murders."

"How does he know that?" Poppy asked.

"He didn't say. And I would never ask him to disclose his sources. But he appears to have a knack for forming prompt alliances with the kitchen staff wherever we go." I shrugged. I was not about to question Wilford's methods. "Do you think someone here would know more?"

"What?! These lunatics?" Poppy cast a derisive

glance at the smattering of white-robed chaps across the lawn. It was clear that Poppy's association with the colony was hurtling towards its inevitable demise. "The only person with any sense who comes here is the local chemist."

I wondered vaguely whether this was also a jab at the members of the Royal Society and was about to take offense on my uncle's behalf. But on second thought, I decided Poppy had the right idea.

"He congratulated me on the excellent job I was doing organizing the denizens of Monte Verita into a productive community," Poppy said, her voice brimming with pride.

As Poppy beamed at the remembered compliment, something in her phrasing made me wonder if the good chemist had bestowed the accolade upon her in the manner doctors in psychiatric wards praise their patients' achievements.

"Have you been able to find out about the books Nicholas and Emmeline, and perhaps Ludovic, were smuggling to Italy? Who was printing them?" I asked. Ludovic's role in all of this was still unclear to me.

I remembered James' assurance that Ludovic was not involved in the murders. Was James' word enough for me? I pursed my lips. James was a decent chap, but even good chaps could be misled.

"The residents here have formed a coalition of sorts," Poppy said crossly, "and refuse to give me any meaningful information."

I patted her on the hand. "What was a chemist doing at Monte Verita?" I asked, trying to distract her from her subordination troubles. The idea of smuggled narcotics was still somewhat fresh in my mind and I couldn't help but make a connection between this chemist and the ease with which he could produce and procure nefarious substances.

"Oh, we had a chap who had run away from a sanatorium in Zurich hiding out at Monte Verita," Poppy said. "It took the residents here a while to figure out that the poor cove was one cracked egg—what with all the other lunatics parading around the community." She threw another disparaging glance at the commune. "But the chap was heavily addicted to morphine and approached the local chemist about it. The chemist, in turn, came to Monte Verita a few times, the last time with the authorities to transport the chap back to Zurich."

We walked in silence for a few minutes. I watched the sun's rays play upon the surface of the lake. The Countess' island was clearly visible from up here, and it made me think of the disconnected clues related to the murders of Emmeline and Nicholas. How did the missing servant girl fit in all of this? What linked all these events?

As though having read my thoughts, Poppy said, "You know the servant girl Wilford alluded to? I wonder if she is somehow connected to the angry man that used to come and shout at the gate…" she trailed off.

"Of course!" I exclaimed, making a few meditating chaps in the vicinity jump. "Wilford said her disappearance was related to the angry man who came to Monte Verita." *Was he responsible for the girl's disappearance or was he angry because she had disappeared?* I wondered. "Have you seen him recently?" I asked Poppy.

She shook her head. "No. And the residents here dismiss him as an unhappy local, troubled by their way of life."

"Did no one talk to him to see what bothered him so much?" I asked. For a group purporting to be enlightened, the Monte Verita people sometimes struck me as inane.

Poppy shrugged. "Well, few of the residents speak Italian," she said, "and those who do apparently could not penetrate the man's obscure dialect."

"So no one could help him?" I asked.

She shook her head.

"Why didn't they enquire in the village?" I pressed on.

"They are not on the best of terms with the village. Apparently there have been some incidents at Monte Verita—a torched sun hut, some ruined crops—that the residents blame on the villages. They think the villagers are trying to drive the colony away. But the villagers are denying any wrong-doing."

"But this man has now stopped coming?" I asked.

"Yes," Poppy answered, narrowing her eyes as though trying to work something out.

"And the disturbances have stopped?"

"Yes. Well, at least there hasn't been an incident since the attack on Lord Packenham," she said. "Though now that you mention it, it is possible that the crazy man attacked Lord Packenham. I wonder why?"

I nodded and thought about the problem at hand. With Monte Verita residents unwilling to talk to us, on account of Poppy, and Ascona villagers weary of foreigners, especially a couple of women known to have frequented Monte Verita, I wondered who could help us find out more about the missing servant girl and her connection to this mystery.

"Do you think the chemist would speak to us?" I asked Poppy.

"I don't see why not," she answered.

Thus, Poppy and I, with the bicycle by my side, proceeded down to Ascona to find the said chemist. An audible sigh of relief trailed us as we crossed the crooked white gates of Monte Verita. Or perhaps I had only imagined it.

"I hope the chemist can throw some light on this. It all sounds so mysterious and complicated," I said as we walked down the winding road.

"You'll figure it out, Gassy. I'm sure of it," Poppy said with more confidence than I felt.

I smiled at Poppy and returned to my thoughts. I'd begun to form an idea about the link between the angry man and the missing girl. I even had an inkling of how she was connected to Ludovic. But I still could not see how her disappearance tied to the murders.

We walked in silence. The village was now just below us.

"Gassy," Poppy turned to me, "do you think I need to remain at Monte Verita now that Nicholas is gone?"

A feeling of gratitude washed over me. Although Poppy's fling with Monte Verita had clearly run its course, she had remained there until the bitter end, simply because I had asked her. And though Poppy shared a lot of character traits with Juan Vicente Gomez, better known as The Tyrant of the Andes, one could not deny that she was a solid chum.

"Of course you don't have to remain up there, if you don't want to," I said, and squeezed her hand to show her my appreciation. "Though I was under the impression that you somewhat like it," I teased.

"I did at the beginning, but I think I'm ready for the comforts of the Grand Hotel Locarno."

CHAPTER 28

The chemist's shop was on a cobbled street just off of the old port. It was a curious shop to have in a fishing village. I propped my bicycle against its gray stone wall. On the outside, two gothic windows greeted the visitor, and on the inside, the shop reminded one of a medieval apothecary.

What little light penetrated the shop glinted off shiny surfaces: the amber glass bottles that lined the dark wood shelves; the small glass vials of the wooden travel boxes displayed on the polished wood counter; the delicate brass scales with their multitude of tiny weights lined up like golden soldiers.

A white marble bust of Paracelsus, the 16th century Swiss physician, took pride of place.

I raised an eyebrow at Poppy. What kind of place was this?

It would not have surprised me if this chemist was hiding an alembic, an aludel and an athanor in the back of the shop. The glass globe filled with red liquid hanging from the vaulted ceiling completed my suspicion that this chemist dabbled in a bit of alchemy.

Would the evidence of such a man be entirely

reliable?

But the small, neat man that emerged from the back of the store belied the store's decor. He wore a crisp white coat and small oval gold-rimmed glasses. His thinning white hair was neatly combed to one side.

He smiled when he saw Poppy, evidently recognizing her.

Poppy made a brief introduction.

"Ah! You are with the English gentlemen who make a daily pilgrimage to Monte Verita," said Herr Pfister. "They are quite singular in their interests." He smiled good-naturedly.

"They are indeed," I agreed.

With the ice thus broken, I jumped right in and asked Herr Pfister about the missing girl.

"Ah, the local young woman who worked at Monte Verita," he said in careful but flawless English. "Yes, I know what happened to her. Though I do not suppose her family would appreciate me sharing her fate with complete strangers." He looked from Poppy to me with a quizzical look. "What interest do two English ladies have in the fate of a local girl?"

"Please, Herr Pfister, we are not asking out of idle curiosity," I protested.

He took a few moments before he answered. "No, I don't think you are," he said. "So, what is your interest in her case?"

"We think it might be related to some recent deaths," I said.

"You mean the English woman who died at the ball in Locarno and the young man who disappeared on the mountain?" he asked.

I nodded. His perception hinted at a sharp mind.

"And there was also the drowning of the young man on the lake," he added, and looked in the direction of the lake, though it was not visible from his apothecary.

"Yes, we were there," Poppy said.

"Were you?" he said and studied us for a moment.

Poppy and I nodded in unison.

"And how do you think the young woman is connected with these tragedies?" he asked. He spoke with a precision akin to measuring out a poisonous compound.

"We're not entirely certain," I said, "but we were hoping you would be able to help us find out." I hoped my candor would disarm him. I might have thrown in a dazzling smile. His reaction reminded me of James—he didn't seem captivated by my charm. "The truth is," I went on, "we're interested in learning more about an Englishman from Monte Verita. I suspect he is at the heart of these deaths."

"I see. And who is this person?" the chemist said.

"At Monte Verita, he was known by the name of Brother Gregor."

The chemist nodded.

"Do you know him?" I asked.

Herr Pfister nodded again and cast his eyes down. "I know him. A troubled young man."

I decided to share with him all I knew about Ludovic, hoping he would reciprocate. "His real name is Ludovic, and he is the son of Lord Packenham. He disappeared from Monte Verita at about the time the young woman, Emmeline, was murdered at the villa. I believe he spent that time hiding at Countess Yablonovna's island—"

"At Isola San Pancrazio?" he asked.

I nodded. As he said nothing else, I resumed my account. "I suspect Ludovic is involved in the murders of Emmeline and Nicholas, but I don't know how or why. Emmeline's murder happened right after Ludovic went missing from Monte Verita, and he reappeared a changed man, groomed and well dressed, in Locarno right after Nicholas fell to his death. Spencer, the man who drowned, Nicholas and Emmeline were involved in smuggling radical books to Italy. Perhaps Ludovic is involved in the smuggling as well. Perhaps the murders are related to the smuggling. But I'm not clear on how the local girl is connected to these events."

Herr Pfister was silent for a few moments, and I could see that he was selecting his words. I waited.

"I can set your mind at ease on a few points," he finally said. "I know the young man well and have had many conversations with him, trying to set him on the right path. It was I who advised him to leave Monte Verita."

"You?" I gasped. "But why?"

"Brother Gregor, or Ludovic as you call him, fell in love with a local girl working as a servant at Monte Verita. And soon after, she was expecting a child." So my suspicions were correct, but I did not interrupt the chemist. "Confused and without friends, the young man turned to me for advice. We'd met on a few occasions at Monte Verita. He confessed that he was brought up in a strict family, and that his father, a rich and powerful man, would not approve of his conduct. He was not against marrying the young woman, Maria, but he dreaded telling his parents about the child."

Herr Pfister paused again, as though to collect his thoughts. "When he unexpectedly saw his father at Monte Verita, I advised him to do the honorable thing. He left for Zurich to set his affairs in order and clean himself up. He was to come back to Locarno in the guise of the gentleman that he was to discuss matters with his father. So you see, he could not have been on the Countess' island, or at the ball, or on the smugglers' trail where the young man fell to his death. Ludovic was in Zurich."

"But what about the girl?" I asked, caught

up in the drama, momentarily pushing aside the ramifications of his revelation.

"Her father sent her to a convent up north to have the child," he said.

"But surely Ludovic plans to marry her!" I exclaimed.

Herr Pfister inclined his head, but I could not interpret his expression.

"So it was her father who kept appearing at the Monte Verita gates, shouting at the residents," I said. "To what purpose?"

"He was angry, understandably. He blamed the whole Monte Verita community for his daughter's misfortune."

"And it was he who caused the fire and other incidents at Monte Verita," I said, hazarding a guess.

Herr Pfister nodded.

"But why didn't he just make Ludovic marry his daughter?" I asked. "Why send her away?"

"In his eyes Ludovic was a worthless young man—living in a radical commune, with no job and no way to support a family. And what's worse, in the father's eyes at least, the young man was not Catholic."

I permitted myself a smile. How wrong Maria's father was. Ludovic was in line to inherit his father's title. Perhaps that would make even Maria's father overlook the young man's transgression regarding his choice of religion.

"And was it Maria's father who attacked Lord Packenham?" I asked.

The chemist nodded.

"But how could he possibly know that Lord Packenham was Ludovic's father?" Poppy asked.

"Pure coincidence, I believe," said Herr Pfister, and he permitted himself a small smile as well.

"I believe Lord Packenham had been going up to Monte Verita not to sneak clandestine looks at the bird, but to look for his son. The two fathers just happened to have run into each other," I said. "They were ignorant of each other's intertwined fates, but both brimming with anger, got into a skirmish." I could see how Lord Packenham could make anyone want to give him a good thrashing. "And do you know if Ludovic plans to marry Maria?" I asked, pulling my mind away from the patriarchal encounter.

"His father has given him his blessing, I believe," Herr Pfister said. "Ludovic should be visiting Maria's father any day now to ask for her hand in marriage."

Oh, to be a fly on the wall when the two families finally met.

CHAPTER 29

Poppy and I discussed the matter of Ludovic's impending nuptials in hushed tones over lunch on the hotel's verandah. But my mind kept drifting to all the questions I still had about Emmeline's and Nicholas' deaths. With Brother Gregor now accounted for, who had strangled Emmeline? Who had been the Englishman hiding out on Countess Yablonovna's island? And had Nicholas' death been an accident, or had he been pushed?

I acknowledged, grudgingly, that James had been correct, and that I should not have doubted his word. I also understood why he could not reveal what he'd known about Ludovic.

But if Ludovic was not the killer, then who was?

Had Nicholas strangled Emmeline for an unknown reason and then faked his own death? It was a satisfactory theory, except that it did not account for the Englishman on the Countess' island. It could not have been Nicholas. At the time, he had been at Monte Verita and then in jail. Then who was the Englishman on the Countess' island? Had the smugglers been mistaken in the man's nationality?

Putting that puzzle piece aside, I wondered why Nicholas had gone to the smuggling trail? Was it to fake his death, to continue smuggling books or to meet someone?

I let my eyes glide over the water as Poppy droned on about golf clubs and handicaps. Apparently, Lord something or other was building a new golf club in the vicinity.

There seemed to be a mysterious figure in the background of these events. There was evidence of him everywhere—the man who frightened Emmeline at the ball, the man on the island, the man who perhaps pushed Nicholas to his death. But who was he?

I'd already been to all the places he'd been—the ball, the island...I faltered. The one place I had not been to was the smuggling trail.

Making my excuses to Poppy and encouraging her to visit the site of the future golf course, I went in search of a messenger boy.

I was certain that at least one boy would have an older brother who knew his way around the smuggling trail. Soon I was surrounded by at least five messenger boys, each professing to have a brother who worked as a smuggler. But only one boy could claim the distinction of having a brother who was a group leader. A group leader guided the men through the forest, negotiated payments with border guards and gave the men a signal to disband when necessary, the boy told me with pride.

Cautiously, I explained to him that I wanted to go to the spot on the trail where the Englishman had fallen.

"You want the Englishman on the trail, yes?" he asked.

"Yes," I nodded. "Can your brother take me to the spot?"

The boy smiled broadly at me. "No problem," he said with confidence. "My brother knows the spot with the Englishman."

Encouraged by the generosity they'd come to expect from me, and with the promise of a handsome payment to the smugglers' leader, the boys sprang into action, and by teatime all was arranged. I was to join this evening's group of smugglers on their excursion to Italy over the mountains.

I wondered if I should tell either Poppy or James about my plans, but ultimately decided that they would either try to stop me or offer to come with me. But I suspected the smugglers would not appreciate the presence of so many foreigners. It had been hard enough to convince them to take me along.

In the end, only my uncle was in a position to figure out my intentions. To complete my transformation into a young chap and blend in with the smugglers, I once again borrowed his golfing plus fours and cap, his hunting socks, and one of his shirts. And I was confident that my uncle would not be able to put all the clues together.

By the time I left his room at the villa with his garments in hand, Uncle Albert was under the impression that I was going owl-watching. I may have played a significant part in helping him formulate this mistaken impression.

Wilford was in a better mental position to guess my intentions, but he was a solid egg and did not interfere with my plans.

The final element of my metamorphosis from a daughter of an English Earl to a young smuggler on the Swiss-Italian border involved meeting the actual smuggling chaps at their assembly point. This evening they were to set off from a grotto tavern on the outskirts of Locarno and proceed from there through the forests and across the hills into Italy.

Getting accepted into the party had proven less tricky than I expected. The messenger boy had supplied me with a glowing reference, on account of all the tips I had given him and his friends during my stay at the Grand Hotel. His brother, the group leader, who happened to speak a bit of English, introduced me to the rest of the chaps.

Our language barrier happily prevented the men from inquiring too much into the reason why I wanted to join their group. A vague description of folklore research exhausted our linguistic prowess and satisfied their curiosity.

Before we could depart on our midnight journey, the men insisted that I should be equipped with the proper footwear.

I would not be a distinguished graduate of Frau Baumgartnerhoff's finishing school if I did not subscribe to the doctrine that proper footwear was essential to the success of any endeavor. Hiking boots, crafted by a shoemaker in the famed village of Zermatt, had kept me on solid ground in Nice, and a pair of handmade boxing shoes had allowed me to sneak about in a villa in Italy. Now, sitting on a granite boulder, I was getting a pair of *peduli* sewn to my feet.

Each of the smugglers wore a pair of these *peduli*. They were nothing more than two fabric sacks, with a tie at the top and no sole, stuffed with wool on the inside. The bottoms of the shoes were stitched with rope to give them traction, and each man helped stitch the bottom of the shoes of his companion. When complete, one's feet resembled two loaves of bread.

I watched enthralled as the group leader stitched my rope soles using a knife to expertly drive the rope through the fabric. He must have interpreted my look as a manifestation of doubt over the shoes' efficacy because he made one of his companions demonstrate how silently the shoes allowed them to navigate the forest floor.

They strapped a woven rucksack called *bricolla*

on my back—if I were to cross the border with them, the leader gesticulated, I might as well carry cargo. Lastly, I noticed that each man carried a knife or even a small sickle as a means of defense. Against what, I wasn't sure. Wild animals, perhaps? All I had was a walking stick.

We filed out of the grotto tavern under cover of darkness and climbed in near silence through the hills for about half an hour. The men clearly knew these woods and the paths well.

As we left the electric lights of the town behind us and plunged into the darkness of the forest, a primal fear overtook me. The near-total darkness animated a dormant instinct. The darkness felt oppressive, and I was keenly aware of the sound of my beating heart. Deprived of my vision, my other senses sharpened. I became alert to the soft steps around me. The men were right—the shoes were nearly silent.

Walking behind the others, I wondered what lay ahead. How far was the place where Nicholas had fallen to his death?

Among the trees, up ahead, I could see a flickering light. As we got closer, the yellow flames of a roaring campfire came into view. The men seemed to have been expecting this and took seats on stumps and rocks around the open fire pit. The flames illuminated the outlines of a stone hut beyond. I wondered vaguely who lived here.

The group leader leaned over to me. "Here lives

the Englishman," he said with the self-satisfied smile of a mission accomplished.

CHAPTER 30

Confusion flooded over me. Where had the smugglers brought me? What Englishman?

I looked around in fear, uncertain as to what would happen next. Was Nicholas still alive and living here?

My brain raced over everything that had transpired between me and the messenger boys. Had they misunderstood me? The boy had said that his brother would bring me to the spot where the Englishman was. But it was not the spot where the Englishman had died...he had meant the spot where the Englishman lived.

The fire crackled, and my heart jumped. Each dry stick snapping in the heat caused me to tense up.

The men sitting round the blaze relaxed and passed around a few bottles of wine. They joked, swapped stories and laughed, resting for the long trek and steep ascent ahead.

I sat in anxious silence among them, staring at the dancing flames of the fire, thinking. Blood drained from my face as the words of the border guard floated up in my mind. He had said that an Englishman had been camping on the smuggling trail...I had assumed it was Nicholas... Fear sharpened my reasoning and disconnected images flashed in my mind's eye: the drowning, the floating ski on the water, Emmeline's talk of ghosts, the man on the island, the charred broken planks in the cold fire on the beach, that I had assumed were from an old boat...

My breathing quickened, like a rabbit ready to spring, every muscle in my body strained, waiting for the Englishman to appear.

I kept glancing towards the hut. Strange shadows from the blaze dance upon its walls, like demons rising from the fire. But the door of the hut remained closed.

And then a man walked out of the shadows of the trees and moved towards the fire. For a brief moment, I hoped to see Nicholas. But I had already guessed that the man would not be him.

The light from the fire illuminated his face, and despite the blaze, a chill passed over me. It was the ghost Emmeline had seen at the villa. Fear paralyzed me. I was in the presence of the killer.

As I gazed upon the man's face from under my cap, and the puzzle pieces joined together, it felt as though the truth had always been in front of me, I had just failed to perceive it. It felt as though deep down I had known the identity of the shadow that had lurked in the background, committing the murders. But I had failed to acknowledge the thought that the only person who could have committed the murders was the drowned man—Spencer.

He had not drowned, but had taken refuge on the island.

I looked at Spencer from under the peak of my cap. The men did not pay him any attention, and for a moment I wondered if I were the only one who could see him. Was he really a ghost?

But the next moment, the leader of the group sitting next to me moved to get Spencer's attention. I pulled his arm back sharply, and he looked at me, confused. I shook my head and pleaded with my eyes to make him understand that I did not want him to introduce me to the Englishman. For a moment he hesitated, but seemed to recognize the fear in my eyes and eased his body back down.

Despite my effort, Spencer stared straight at me. Had he recognized me? If he had, he didn't show it. His stony silence was frightening. If I was correct, he had already killed two people. What was he planning for me?

I pulled the hat over my face, but that only made my hair slip out of the back. I tried to sink into the shadows. I could hear the blood pumping in my ears.

What was I to do? Could I alert the smugglers? But I didn't speak Italian. And even if I could communicate my suspicions to them, would they believe me? They were Spencer's friends.

I could slip back and return to the town on my own. But would I get lost in this darkness? Would Spencer follow me?

I was probably safer sticking with the group. Perhaps Spencer would not join the smugglers on their trek tonight.

As the men continued to chat, my thoughts crystalized and recollections flooded back.

The man Emmeline had seen at the party had been Spencer. That was the reason she had been so frightened and confused at the party. She'd thought he was dead.

Why had she been frightened and not happy to see him alive? Had she wanted him dead? Did she think Nicholas had drowned Spencer?

But something had gone wrong. Nicholas had said so to Emmeline. Emmeline's panic on the beach was not because Spencer had drowned, but because Nicholas could not be certain that Spencer had drowned.

Before I could make sense of it all, the smugglers rose and prepared to continue their trek. A man helped me with my rucksack.

I had a decision to make. Should I continue with the men, or should I slip back to Locarno and let the police know Spencer was alive?

Hesitating, I sidled to the end of the line. If I decided to go back, all I had to do was turn back and let the electric lights of the town below be my guide.

But that was not the safest decision. Surely, the safest option was to stay with the group. My only aim now was to stay alive. I would have to follow through with the smuggling trek.

As the fire was doused and its light went out with a hiss, we were once again plunged into darkness.

I listened for the men's voices and footsteps ahead of me, and followed them.

We walked for a long while, deep into the forest, ever ascending. Italy was over the crest. I did not know if Spencer had joined the file.

After a while, everything became quiet. Had I lost the group? I stopped and listened. How could I have lost them? Had I been so absorbed in my thoughts?

In a moment, I knew what must have happened. I had been following the person in front of me and the person had led me away from the group. I was now on my own with a killer.

I clutched my walking stick. Fear overtook me. I heard a faint step near me. And suddenly, Frau Baumgartnerhoff's training came back to me. I took a deep breath to calm my beating heart. I stood in silence in the forest, listening for my opponent's first move.

The darkness amplified my sense of hearing.

The slight rustle of a shirt to my left prompted me to bring my stick up in the outside lateral position, ready to strike.

What my opponent didn't know was that I had been carrying a walking stick fashioned out of quebracho wood. A tree species found in the forests of Paraguay and Argentina, the wood was some of the hardest in the world. If my opponent were to attack me, he would soon discover the reason the Spanish settlers named this tree the "ax-breaker".

The second thing my opponent didn't know was that Frau Baumgartnerhoff, a divorced woman, living on her own with a large number of young ladies in her care, had educated each and everyone of her charges in the art of cane fighting.

A form of self-defense made popular in France during the 19th century, Frau Baumgartnerhoff considered cane fighting an essential skill for ladies about to foray into society. The skill was easily concealed, but at a moment's notice, a lady's parasol or walking stick could be turned into a weapon.

My walking stick had the further advantage of having a square shape, with edges sharpened to deliver the utmost damage to my opponent.

I heard the tread of my adversary to my left. He was about to strike. I blocked his blow, his own wooden club shattering against mine, then tucked and rolled out of his strike zone.

The rustle of his garments and the breaking of a tree limb told me he was about to lunge at me again, this time on my right. I flipped the point of my cane behind me, ready to deliver a blow, if calculated accurately, to his head.

But as I executed my swing, I failed to connect with his head. I had either miscalculated my strike, or, more likely, my opponent was not a stranger to the art of cane fighting. My brain reminded me that Spencer was an accomplished athlete.

I applied thrusting dives to hit Spencer in the belly or face, and used circular trajectories to swipe him off his feet. But my cane connected with his body only occasionally and didn't seem to deliver lasting damage to my assailant.

With both of us capering around the forest floor, with blows and lunges delivered at lightning speed in the darkness and with the incessant shattering of heavy branches against my walking stick, I soon became disoriented. Instead of striking, I assumed defense positions and practiced evasive maneuvers.

Unexpectedly, a blow connected vertically with my shoulder. My assailant had armed himself with yet another branch. Though his stick was not as lethal as mine, the force of the strike was enough to discompose me. As pain seared through my body, my opponent delivered a horizontal strike to my head and brought me to the forest floor.

Head swimming, I rolled out of the way with difficulty and his next strike missed. But I was uncertain as to how long I could continue fighting in the darkness. With renewed will, quieting the rushing blood in my head, I jumped to my feet.

Then, in the distance, I saw lights moving among the trees. Voices threaded through the forest. A group was moving our way. But I could not let my attention waver. I leaped to the side and switched places with my opponent, so that he was now illuminated by the torches of the people coming our way.

As light flashed across his face, I knew he would be momentarily distracted and delivered an outside lateral strike to his neck. Spencer crumbled to the ground.

CHAPTER 31

"So Nicholas' body has not yet been recovered?" Poppy asked.

It was a few days after Spencer had been arrested for the murder of Emmeline and the presumed murder of Nicholas.

"It may never be," Mr. Linnaeus said. "More than one person has been lost to the steep cliffs of the Alps. But bringing up the bodies is sometimes too dangerous, so they are left to rest forever in the bosom of the Alps."

I thought back to the night in the forest. My body could have joined those unfortunate souls had not rescuers come to my aid. But I'd been rescued not by the smugglers, as I had assumed at the time, but by the police.

Coming down the mountain with them, I'd wondered who had alerted the police and how they'd managed to arrive just in the nick of time. At first I had assumed that the police were following the smuggling gang, and considered their timely appearance a lucky coincidence. But it transpired that their presence in the forest that night had a more inspired genesis.

While I had assured Uncle Albert that I needed

to borrow his clothes for some late-night owling, preceded by a spell of lighthearted scavenger hunting with Poppy and some chums from the Grand Hotel, he had not entirely believed me. The nature of my escapades in France and Italy had tipped him off, and he raised his concerns with Wilford.

Wilford, in turn, had placed a telephone call to the Grand Hotel, where he'd conversed with a baffled Poppy, who during their brief exchange had taken an increasing offense that she had not been invited to this game of owl hunting. And she'd lamented loudly that she took issue with being cast aside for some new group of friends I had formed.

These were all the clues Wilford required to devise a scavenger hunt plan of his own. He visited the Grand Hotel, and soon the messenger boy who had been my connection to the smuggling gang had been smoked out and my coordinates established. Wilford had also correctly deduced that my subterfuge was probably related to the murder of Emmeline and the disappearance of Nicholas. This had enticed the local police into action.

As I had helped catch a killer, my involvement in the contraband enterprise that night was overlooked, and no smuggling charges were brought against me.

We were sitting in Mr. Linnaeus' beautiful

gardens for afternoon tea. Even though birds were chirping and exotic butterflies were flitting here and there, for once the attention of the members of the Royal Society was not distracted by such things.

"What made you suspect that Spencer was behind the murders?" Poppy asked.

"I didn't," I said. "I believed he'd drowned. Seeing him in the forest that night was like seeing a ghost. Although, deep down, I probably always suspected that there was something strange about his drowning. But I couldn't put my finger on it. I'd seen and heard clues about him—the burned ski plank on the Countess' beach, for example—but I didn't put them all together until it was too late."

"Then why did you go to the forest in the first place?" asked Poppy.

"I wanted to see where Nicholas had fallen and I wondered what had made him go on the smuggling trail." I said and shrugged. "Plus, I had some suspicion that perhaps Nicholas was still alive. His body had not been recovered, so I could not dismiss the possibility that he was still alive."

I sipped tea for a few moments, collecting my thoughts.

"Yet, the theory that he was Emmeline's killer was not fully satisfactory," I said. "I knew for certain that the person who had been hiding out at the Countess' island could not have been Nicholas —he was at Monte Verita. I'd suspected Brother

Gregor, Ludovic, but it could not have been him either." I threw James a furtive look.

I did not need to elaborate for the present company why Ludovic was not a suspect. While Lord Packenham and Ludovic were not partaking in afternoon tea with us, their story had already been properly ventilated by the Royal Society. There was no need to repeat the details.

I turned my thoughts back to the case. From the beginning I'd made the mistake of assuming that three men and one woman were involved in this mystery—Spencer, Nicholas, Ludovic and Emmeline. Once I'd eliminated Ludovic and all the distracting details—his disappearance, the attack on Lord Packenham, the angry local hurling insults at the Monte Verita residents, the missing servant girl—three questions remained. Who had frightened Emmeline at the party? Who had been on the Countess' island? And who had pushed Nicholas to his death?

I had realized, perhaps too late, that if I could answer those questions, I would know who Emmeline's killer was. And Spencer was the answer to these three questions.

"So, who was hiding on the island?" my uncle asked.

"Spencer," I said. Though Uncle Albert nodded, his eyes were glazed with uncertainty.

"But what was it all about? Why was Emmeline killed? And if Spencer hadn't drowned, what was he doing hiding on the island to begin with?" Mr. Linnaeus asked.

Between Poppy's visits to the police station with freshly baked cakes and Wilford's visits to the hotel's kitchens, the story of what had happened had emerged.

"It all began as a lover's triangle," I said. "Spencer and Emmeline had married in England. The little inheritance she had, after she was disowned by her family for her unorthodox life, she squandered on a lavish bohemian existence. And by that point, her family had little left anyway, having had to pay for the families involved in the various industrial accidents.

"Emmeline and her husband made their way to Europe, traveled, and heard about Monte Verita. It was everything Emmeline was looking for— freedom from the establishment, away from the eyes of English society, and a chance to spread her radical ideas to Italy. The rise of Mussolini and his brutal oppression of the workers of the country elicited strong passions in her. Emmeline truly believed in the socialist and communist ideas and ideals, and threw herself wholeheartedly into printing and smuggling literature into Italy."

Since Spencer's arrest, we'd been able to track down in Bellinzona the printer who had supplied the underground literature. A nice chap, though a bit fanatical. He had helped shed some light on Emmeline's character and motivations.

"But then she met Nicholas at Monte Verita," I continued. "He possessed all the qualities that she believed Spencer lacked. While she had married Spencer for his brawn, he did not possess the intellectual prowess of Nicholas. She became deeply attracted to Nicholas' ideas and then to his person.

"Nicholas had figured out who Emmeline was, but despite her family's role in the death of his own family members, he didn't hold a grudge against her. He began falling in love with her and never revealed his true identity."

I paused once more to take a sip of tea. From here on, the story was built on supposition and the little Spencer had disclosed to the police.

"I cannot be sure when Nicholas and Emmeline hatched the plan to get rid of Spencer," I said. "Emmeline had probably tried to push Spencer away, but he was not going anywhere. While Spencer lacked her passion for the cause, he was happy enough to do her bidding. He was probably attracted to her personality and didn't want to leave her. He participated wholeheartedly in the smuggling of books and became friendly with the other smugglers on the trail. That's why they never questioned his presence on the island or at the hut on the trail."

"But why didn't the smugglers report him? Didn't they know that he was supposed to be dead?" Lord Dodsworth asked, shocked by the indifference of the locals towards this whole affair.

"The smugglers are gone for days at a time on the trail. They probably didn't realize that it was Spencer who was supposed to be dead. All they had probably heard was that a man from Monte Verita had drowned. They would have had no reason to suspect that Spencer was that man. As Countess Yablonovna said, smugglers keep to themselves and try to avoid contact with the authorities." I shrugged. "Though they knew him by sight, I doubt if they knew Spencer's name."

"So what happened on the day of the drowning?" Alistair asked. Having been present that day, he was probably keen to understand how Spencer's deception had worked.

"Perhaps Nicholas and Emmeline had discussed ways to get rid of Spencer by making his death look like an accident," I said. "The day of the waterskiing outing, Nicholas recognized such an opportunity. When Nicholas stopped the boat in an area with lake weed, Spencer began sinking, and his skis got tangled in the weeds. Seeing Spencer struggle to get back to the boat, Nicholas seized his chance. Spencer and Nicholas were evenly matched physically, but Nicholas had an advantage over Spencer, who had his feet tied to the ski boards. Nicholas pushed Spencer under the water and planned to keep him there until he drowned. Spencer fought back. From the shore, their struggle looked as though Nicholas was desperately trying to help the drowning Spencer, while, in fact, he was trying to keep him under the water."

The faraway looks on Poppy's and James' faces told me they were trying to recollect the events they had witnessed that day.

"But Spencer was not as doltish as Emmeline believed him to be, as he proved by his subsequent actions," I continued. "He understood what was going on, that Nicholas was trying to drown him, and dove underwater, out of his reach. Remember how Nicholas was looking frantically around the boat, as though trying to locate Spencer?" I asked, turning to Poppy and James, and the secretaries who had been with us that day.

James nodded. "He was not searching for him because he believed he had drowned. He was searching for him because he was sure he had not completed the job of drowning him."

"That's right," I said. "Spencer went under water, untied one of his skis, the one the police found floating nearby, and kept the other to help him swim to the Countess' island. He swam underwater at first, and once far enough from the boat, came up for air. He knew of the smugglers stopping on the island. It was easy for him to steal some clothes—the gardener's—and stay on the island for a few days, doing some light gardening work."

The Countess had confirmed that the old

gardener had grumbled about things going missing on the island. But she had originally dismissed his complaints as forgetfulness due to his age.

"But why did Nicholas and Emmeline want to kill Spencer? What did they have to gain?" asked Alistair.

"Nicholas would have Emmeline to himself. But I think there was also another reason they wanted to kill him. For the insurance. Emmeline didn't have money, but Spencer's life was insured. If they could stage an accident, they would get the insurance money," I explained. "They had big plans for Nicholas' ideas."

"But they ran into a snag," James said.

"That's right," I said. "Without Spencer's body, they could not claim the insurance."

"Was it Spencer who had frightened Emmeline at the ball?" Mr. Linnaeus asked. "Did he come to the ball with the intention of killing Emmeline?"

"He denies it," Poppy said. As our ambassador to the local police station, she was in possession of the most current information about Spencer's account of the events. "At first he had thought that only Nicholas was responsible for trying to kill him. But Emmeline's reaction to his reappearance at the ball, alive, left him in no doubt of her feelings on the matter. She was not happy to see him alive and well."

"And of course there was also Nicholas'

reaction," I added. "It was only later that I began to question why he would not say who Emmeline had seen at the ball? If the drowning had been an accident, why hide that Spencer had survived and was alive? The only explanation was that Nicholas was hiding his own guilt. Nicholas could not say anything about Spencer because Spencer would accuse Nicholas of attempted murder."

"So what was Spencer's motive for the murders?" Mr. Linnaeus asked.

"Love and money, I think," I said. "Spencer went to the ball to tell Emmeline what Nicholas had done, but discovered that she was in on it. So, in his rage, he murdered her. He then remembered that he could benefit from her death—he was the beneficiary of her life-insurance policy—if he could stage it as an accident."

"The fan," Mr. Linnaeus said.

I nodded. "Flimsy, but Spencer probably realized only after that he needed to make Emmeline's death look like an accident. It was the best he could do at the time."

"But surely he could not claim her life insurance?" Poppy protested. "He was supposed to be dead!"

"He can't claim it now that he has been arrested for her murder, but he could have before," I said. "With Nicholas and Emmeline both dead, and the local police suspecting some unidentified lunatic with a vendetta against Monte Verita as the culprit, Spencer could have lived under an assumed identity for a while and then reappear as himself a few years later. He could claim that he had suffered from amnesia," I suggested.

"Like the Count of Monte Cristo," my uncle said.

"Yes, I suppose," I said. "Though slightly less complicated." By the look in my uncle's eyes, I could see that he did not agree.

"And since everyone believed his disappearance was a tragic accident," James added, "the authorities would have no reason to suspect him as the person behind the deaths of Emmeline and Nicholas. He would have no motive for killing Emmeline. He was her devoted husband."

"And how did Spencer kill Nicholas?" asked Alistair.

"He lured him to the smuggling trail," I said. "Or perhaps Nicholas himself went to investigate. Remember, Nicholas knew Spencer was alive. He heard that an Englishman was living on the smuggling trail. Perhaps he went to confront him about Emmeline's murder."

"Or perhaps he went to kill Spencer," Poppy said. "I think Nicholas was afraid for his life. That's why he didn't object when the police arrested him. He liked being in jail. He was safe there from Spencer."

"And the ski? What happened to the ski?" my uncle piped up.

I smiled at Uncle Albert's very astute question.

Had I noticed the ski in the first place, I might have guessed sooner that Spencer was still alive. "It ended up on a bonfire on the Countess' island. I just didn't recognize it at the time."

"But the thing that clinched Spencer's guilt was my camera," Poppy said, placing the apparatus on the table.

She was correct. The police had discovered the camera in the hut on the smuggling trail. It was irrefutable evidence that Spencer had been at Mr. Linnaeus' party.

"Though I wish he had not exposed my film," she lamented. "Perhaps we can take another trip with the omnibus through the mountains," she said, and turned to me.

I shook my head most vehemently.

Uncle Albert and I took an evening stroll on the promenade along the lake. Lord Packenham was walking towards us. In front of him, walking hand in hand, were his son Ludovic and his new wife Maria. In front of them, a nanny was pushing a pram.

Lord Packenham and Uncle Albert exchanged nods. Uncle Albert was quite keen on seeing the baby, but I had told him that Lord Packenham needed time to adjust to his new position.

None of the members of the Royal Society held

Ludovic's actions against Lord Packenham. After all, the Society's charter dictated it confine itself to discussing lizards and other such things, not other people's moral virtue.

But Lord Packenham was perhaps his own harshest critic. Having spent his whole life meting out rectitude points to all those around him, he could not fathom that other people would not judge him as harshly as he'd judged them.

And had his son done anything so wrong? He had fallen in love and now had a young family. I smiled at the couple as we passed each other.

Having reached the end of the promenade, Uncle Albert and I turned back towards the Grand Hotel. Our trunks were packed, and my uncle was already looking forward to our journey on the sleeper train tonight. He was especially excited about the twenty-minute trip under the mighty Alps through the Gotthard tunnel. Hopefully, we would reach England the next day, if a beetle did not cross our path.

THE END

THANK YOU FOR READING A BODY IN THE VILLA

A Body in the Villa is book 3
of the Lady Caroline Murder Mysteries.

For more Lady Caroline adventures,
visit the series's page:
Lady Caroline Murder Mysteries

If you would like to to access this book's
Historical Notes, to learn more about the
historical tidbits that made it into the book,
such as Monte Verita, poverty and smuggling
in 1920s Switzerland, why so many aristocrats
populated the British Diplomatic Service, the
perils of driving through Switzerland in the
1920s, what meeting was held in Lady Caroline's
conference room at Grand Hotel Locarno in
1925, and a lot more, visit my website:
https://isabellabassett.com

There, you can learn more about the

Lady Caroline series, or sign up for my emails, get in touch with me, learn about the other mystery series I write, or read about beautiful Switzerland, where I live.

MORE BOOKS BY ISABELLA BASSETT:

The Lady Caroline Murder Mysteries, a 1920s historical mysteries series about a London 'it' girl compelled to be her batty uncle's secretary.

Book 1: Murder at the Grand Hotel
Book 2: Death in the Garden
Book 3: A Body in the Villa
The series continues

The Old Bookstore Mysteries series about an old Swiss bookstore with a peculiar black cat.

Book 1: Out of Print
Book 2: Murderous Misprint
Book 3: Suspicious Small Print
Book 4: Reckless Reprint
Book 5: Incriminating Imprint
Book 6: Scandalous Snow Print
Book 7: Blackmail Blueprint
The series continues